Paul Sayer

Paul Sayer was born and brought up in South Milford, near Leeds. He worked as a staff nurse in a large psychiatric hospital, before becoming a full-time writer. THE COMFORTS OF MADNESS, his first novel, was the Whitbread Book of the Year in 1988, since when he has written three further novels, HOWLING AT THE MOON, THE ABSOLUTION GAME and THE STORM-BRINGER. His work has been translated into seven languages, and he lives with his wife and son in York.

SCEPTRE

The
Storm-Bringer

PAUL SAYER

SCEPTRE

First published in Great Britain in 1994 by Constable
First published in paperback in 1995 by Hodder and Stoughton
A Division of Hodder Headline PLC
A Sceptre Paperback

10 9 8 7 6 5 4 3 2 1

British Library Cataloguing in Publication Data

Sayer, Paul
    Storm Bringer. – New ed
    I.Title
    823.914 [F]

    ISBN 0 340 63495 2

Typeset by Hewer Text Composition Services, Edinburgh
Printed and bound in Great Britain by
Cox & Wyman Ltd, Reading, Berks.

Hodder and Stoughton
A Division of Hodder Headline PLC
338 Euston Road
London NW1 3BH

Acknowledgments

I would like to thank the Society of Authors and the Authors' Foundation for their financial assistance in the writing of this book.

The passage on page 67 is an adaptation from *The Life and Death of Margaret Clitherow*, edited by William Nicholson (1926).

I have tried to be faithful in my descriptions of York and its surrounding areas, though some of the places described are entirely fictional. The room in the Minster, described on pages 143–145, does not exist and the village of Little Pawnton will not be found on any map. All the characters are, of course, simply products of my imagination.

P.S.

To Colin, John and Delia

∫

It had become a favourite walk for Myra and John: through the streets to the river, by a litter-strewn tower and the railings of the Museum Gardens, crossing over at the first bridge then back at the next. From there they might continue past tall handsome terraced houses and St George's Field to the smaller homes, even out to the countryside if they thought it might please them. It had never failed to charm Myra since their arrival here in winter, in flight, six months before. But today she noticed little of the life around her, not the white boats on the water, not the golden light of early autumn. She was locked in a vacuum with her husband, a glass bubble that contained them both, Myra and John, quiet with each other, not touching.

It was always like this when Myra had something new to suggest. And it was nothing really, a modest idea for change, a way of opening up their lives a little, no more. But her possession of it, still unsaid, was making her heavy, almost dizzy, indeed like some pregnant thing who might ask a passer-by for help up the bridge steps. It seemed childish that such a slight wish should cause her this anxiety. But Myra knew the past had made John a fragile creature, friendly enough to all who met him, but with a centre she knew to be brittle, unfixed. The glass bubble was his. It was where he chose to stay.

They walked slowly on among the Sunday afternoon crowds, Myra feeling ungainly at John's side, more conscious than usual that she was the taller of the two. She glanced at him now and then, watching the closed expression, the grey eyes as he stared vacantly at the small park they had reached, at the busy roads, at the lop-sided mound of Clifford's Tower, and the Eye of York, this York, proud and fiercely northern. Now Myra was wearying of the idea in her head, as if it were an old burden to which she felt only a dry sense of duty. If it were to have any valid life she would have to let it out, let it take its chance for survival on the warm afternoon air.

She stopped. And John stopped too, without question.

'A lodger,' Myra said. 'What would you think?'

Not the words she had meant to use. Already she was making a hash of it.

'What?'

'I mean, what would you think? About the idea of taking in a lodger?'

Direct. Better.

'Who, us?'

'Yes.'

John frowned, one eye closed as he scratched his temple. He smiled.

'I don't know. Don't know what I'd think. Can't say I've ever thought of such a thing.'

'Well, would you think about it?'

He shrugged.

'I could, I suppose. If you wanted me to.'

'I think I do. It's an idea I've had, that's all. A way of making a little money.'

'Do we need more money?'

'Probably not. But it would help. And it would be something for me to do.'

John looked down at the cobbles of the riverside walk, testing their fastness with the heel of his shoe. He was completely unmoved, Myra knew that, watching him standing there, hands in pockets, the repeated flexion of his wrists betraying an instant impatience with the idea.

'When did you think this up?'

'I don't know when. I don't think when matters. I thought of it. I have a lot of time to think, as you know,' said Myra, her reserve thinning now the initial confrontation was over.

John looked across the river at a new block of flats, the Sea Cadet headquarters, an old warehouse that had been converted into a restaurant and bar.

'I don't know,' he said.

He didn't know. A cloud of starlings swooped into the trees behind them, children were tumbling on the warm grass or queuing for ice cream, couples strolled arm-in-arm, possessed by each other, a barge chugged by, exquisitely ornate in red and gold, its passengers smiling, everyone smiling, with lives to be lived, contentment to be sought, perhaps already achieved and simply to be savoured. And John did not know. Typically. Couldn't he see they had to do something? To move their lives on a step? After what they had been through, didn't he realise they must move forward? And why was it always Myra who had to take the lead? Hadn't she suffered too?

Now he looked bored, standing there in his light cotton jacket, the one Myra would have to prompt him to change for his thick tweed one when the weather turned cooler. He wore the same jacket every day of the week, often with the same baggy twill trousers and brogues he was wearing now. Myra had once met some of his colleagues at a function at the architect's offices where he worked. Unlike John, they were a sharply dressed lot – blue suits, spiv ties, red braces. Maybe it was only the eighties power look, but it was still smart, still regarded in the North. It amazed Myra that the head of the firm had never pulled John up about his appearance. But then maybe he didn't feel it necessary, disarmed perhaps by John's previous professional experience, or the good looks that his near-shabbiness artfully enhanced. Next year he would be forty, but it would not alter his looks – no grey to appear in the fine mousy hair, no browning of the little strawberry mark beneath his eye. Physically, he had stopped ageing at thirty-five when Myra, two years younger, felt she had overtaken him, crashing towards middle age the way women did, though it rarely bothered her.

'So,' he said, grinning. 'A lodger.'

'Think of it as having a house guest if the word "lodger" doesn't appeal.' A rehearsed line, leaden in its arrival. But she needed to press the subject on him, to force his interest. 'John, it would be good for me. I need to feel useful again. It's all right for you, you've got work.'

'And so have you.'

'When it's around I have. I've worked two weeks since we came here. If I could find a regular job I'd take it.'

'Yes, I know. I'm sorry.'

In tacit agreement they began walking back, the last few minutes seeming like a huge shift in time to Myra. Her idea was on the agenda and she felt better, outside the bubble, the sweet air rushing in to deliver her. But John was still locked in there, alone, with no apparent thought for escape.

The town was as busy as on any weekday, the traffic moving thick and slow over Ouse Bridge, the crowds idling away the hours. A queue of people had gathered by a glass-topped pleasure boat, wearing jeans, pastel tops, the over-sized T-shirts that were a kindness to all body shapes, and a few pairs of shorts, remnants of a decent summer. And all was life, and all was good. But John saw none of it. Myra looked down at the ground, at her summer dress with the prized frivolity of its red rabbit motifs. This, alas, like John's jacket, would soon have to be put away for the winter.

They stopped outside a wine bar while one of a gang of young drinkers took a photograph for a Japanese couple. Myra looked at the fixed smiles of the two tourists, trying to guess their ages. Eighteen? Thirty? Then she looked boldly at John who was also watching them, frowning, as if he were wishing they had asked him to take the picture to give him something to do. When it was over, the Japanese man took his camera back explaining that they were here for the history, and to improve their English. This last comment brought bantering from the photographer's friends about his having hardly learned the language himself, even though he'd lived here all his life. The Japanese man laughed excessively and entered into an innocent conversation about their tour of Europe.

'Do you want a drink?' asked Myra.

'Sorry?'

'Here? We could go in here, if you like.'

'No,' he said. 'I don't want a drink.'

Brood then, thought Myra.

They walked up the worn stone steps of the bridge and into the town, a rare diversion, John leading the way as if to take the old route was for some reason unthinkable.

Here the air was cool in the shadows, the crowds thinner, parents holding on to tired children while they looked in the windows of closed shops. On a sunny corner of the street, in a bank doorway, a laughing bedraggled man was playing an accordion. He had a dog with him which barked at certain points in the music, amusing those passing by, including Myra who went over to toss a coin in the hat on the pavement. John failed to notice the gesture, walking on ahead. Myra bit her lip, hanging back to see how far he would go before he stopped, wondering if he would make it all the way home before he realised she was not at his side.

Eventually, at the square at the end of the street, John did turn round, smiling, arms held wide in apology. Myra caught up with him and he put his arm around her shoulder.

'Sorry. Miles away,' he said, alert now, looking around and nodding at a small café just off the square. 'Do you want to go in there? To talk, I mean.'

'All right,' said Myra.

The café was old-fashioned in that it had neither the fakery of an olde-worlde tea room nor the brashness of a fast-food place. With its marbled tiled walls and round pine tables it looked as if it had been started in – and not improved since – the early part of the last decade. The only other customers were three mackintoshed elderly people who took Myra and John's entry as a cue that they might leave, relieved of their duty in being the establishment's sole supporters.

The girl behind the counter was pretty and sullen, and she worked the coffee machine absent-mindedly. John nudged Myra's arm, gesturing towards a glass case containing solitary pastries. Myra shook her head and went to sit down. When John joined her the girl turned up the volume on a muzak machine behind the counter, changing tapes, winding the new one forward until she found a track that interested her. It was an old soul song to which she mouthed some of the words. Perhaps, Myra thought idly, it was her secret dream to be a singer, or an actress, to have a life beyond all this. Or maybe she had more practical ambitions for owning property, running a night-club, a department store, being her own man. Or maybe none of these things. After half a minute of the soul song she wound the tape on to some furious electronic dance music which, for all its energy, left her uninspired. She turned the volume half-down again and stared out at the sun-drenched street with John, a connoisseur of vulgar behaviour, watching her, smiling.

'Well,' he said, turning to Myra. 'How much thought have you actually given to this idea of yours?'

This idea of yours. Already he was using it against her, making sure she would be responsible if things went wrong.

'Plenty. Lots of people do it round here.'

'Do they?'

'Come on, you know they do. Students, nurses, they're always looking for somewhere to live in a town like this. And as I said, it would give me an interest in life. I want something of my own, John. Something I can control. We came here for your job, remember? For all kinds of reasons . . .' She watched for any change of expression and seeing none felt bold enough to carry on. 'It's hardly asking the earth. And it needn't be on any grand scale. I did my sums the other day. Ideally, we'd need three to make it pay – '

'Three?'

'Let me finish. We could try with one. Make it clear from the start that it's a new venture for us. Set a time limit. Three months, one month even. And if it didn't work out we could soon get rid of whoever we got. The law's on the landlord's side these days, not like when we were students.'

She paused, drying up, the detailed argument she had been preparing for days eluding her. It all sounded rather paltry and she could sense the girl trying to listen above the music, contemptuous perhaps for the modest scale of Myra's ambitions.

John sipped his coffee and sat back, hands resting limply

in his lap. Myra took a packet of cigarettes from her bag and lit one, leaving the packet open on the table. John reached for it then resisted the urge, letting his hand drop to his side.

'We already have a lodger,' he said.

'What do you mean?'

'Long thin tail. Furry. Pointy ears, or maybe I imagined those. Saw it the other day, helping itself to the butter.' He craned his head forward to read the 'Get Stuffed' menu in the centre of the table. 'A mouse.'

'Don't change the subject.'

'We'll have to set a trap.'

'John, please?'

He sat forward, elbows on the table, making a steeple with his fingers.

'The house isn't ours to let.'

'That wouldn't matter, and you know it.'

'All right, maybe I just don't want anyone else round the place.'

'But you're out all day. And three could easily lose themselves in a house that big. John, I'm going mad in there. I don't know anyone round here.'

Myra stopped herself, sensing yet one more impasse, another rift bringing their whole seven years together up for inspection, all along the line from that moment when she had first met him at that awful party in Manchester, John, the quiet one in the corner, a sophisticate, not wanting to dance, but blessed with graceful conversation, heart-melting courtesy. Then there was the first night out, and the next, and the lovemaking and the moment when Myra knew she had scored heftily. Bull's-eye. Their personalities were two halves of a circle, they were meant for each other, almost too perfectly suited. And there was all the time that followed, the wedding four months later, the nights and days of love when Myra remembered looking at him asleep, thinking he had been sent to *save* her, though from what she did not know. Good times, then the not so good . . . All they had been through, all along the line. It struck Myra as unthinkable that everything, this all, the good small society that had been their marriage could ever be in jeopardy. Perhaps her idea was too much, too threatening, and she should back down . . .

The end of the electronic music surprised them both. The girl switched off the machine and resumed her watch on the street. Now Myra's drawing on the cigarette and the creak of John's chair were the only sounds in the room.

'Couldn't you have told me before?' he said, frowning. 'I mean . . .'

'Before what? I'm telling you now. Listen, I know things have been difficult,' Myra said, glancing at the girl and taming her voice to a whisper. 'But we have to put it all behind us. There has to be change. Life will get better if we make the effort. Trust me. John, I want to do this.'

He was looking at the girl whose face, since she could plainly hear everything, had softened with her interest in the state of play.

'Well,' said John, folding his arms. 'All right. A trial period. If you're sure it's what you want.'

'I am. It's a good idea. I know it is,' she said, though the effort of her argument had begun to make her doubt herself. She reached for his hand, squeezing it to reassure him, to reassure herself against the small guilt she was feeling over this triumph of insistence. But he pulled it away.

'It's OK,' he said. 'It's all right.'

Outside, the street musician was passing, humping the heavy accordion, the dog skittering around his ankles. Perhaps, thought Myra, he was looking for a better pitch, somewhere else where people sought the history of this town, this York, where she and John were seeking a new history for themselves.

2

The move to York had been their second upheaval in twelve months, the first having been born of a paler imperative.

Then they were living in Manchester, which both of them were tiring of; Myra had been there since her student days, John for most of his life. Maybe they only wanted a change, but they seemed to need a reason for it, an external logic to justify a new life. So they turned to crime – joy-riding, ram-raiding, a shooting in Moss Side. The bad news that had always been there came anew, fuelling the cult of change in their minds. And when Myra found hypodermics in their suburban front garden John was impressively sickened. 'It's like a cancer,' he said. 'Like America.' Myra agreed. It was no place for them, no place for a child. And each new reported crime gave the idea of moving an irresistible impetus, making them blind to the genuinely good heart of the city, its mood for renewal.

They explored the possibilities, discounting life in another town, making weekend visits to the powerful spaces of the Pennines. This inspired a heady fantasy about owning and living off a small stretch of land, forging an intimacy with the earth. But in her more realistic moments Myra knew this should stay a dream, remembering friends who had gone in pursuit of such a fashionable idyll, only to be disappointed by the emptiness of the countryside, to have it draw them out of themselves, reduce them to the shadows they followed across the grassy hills in search of fading romantic notions. Yet despite this rationality, the wish remained, a law of nature that must be obeyed, if only in a compromised fashion.

'A move then,' said Myra. 'The country. But not the "good life". We're not suited to it.'

John laughed. They agreed that he would keep his job – he was too successful, too capable – while Myra would leave teaching, if only for a while. And so they went, in spring, in hope, with the nights light and clear, their hearts made big with optimism.

And a year later they were here in York, in a future that seemed to have constructed itself without their consent, according to its own wayward laws . . .

'Single room?'

The second time he had said it.

Myra looked down at the blue nylon holdall he had set on the step. She turned on the porch light and he blinked theatrically, the face young and large, cheeks red with the rain, full wide lips, eyes glassy blue. His hair was damp and matted, short at the sides in a modern fierce style, but it was badly attended to, growing out into a parody of the original design. His grubby sheepskin coat covered broad shoulders, a proud chest, and all about him was an aura of stocky strength, the conceit of good health that was a preserve of the young.

'Your ad,' he said. 'In the paper.'

'Yes?'

'You've a room to rent.'

'Of course. I'm sorry.'

'Well?'

In the lounge the radio was still on, though John might not be listening now, perhaps preferring to stand by the door to hear what Myra and the caller were saying. The advertisement had been in the local paper for two weeks and until this moment there had been no response. Myra had not consulted John over its wording and as far as she knew he had not even seen it, though he did ask casually about it after the first two days. Since then he had not mentioned it, perhaps secretly hoping Myra would tire of the idea of taking in a paying guest. And indeed the waiting, and the silence it had induced among the paper's readers, had made Myra question her own enthusiasm for the project. Certainly for the last week she had not bothered to buy the paper and check its entry, feeling a vague embarrassment about its lying there on the page, an impertinence, a touting for business by a newcomer in a town that did not want to know her. And now, faced with the sudden appearance of this man, Myra was oddly regretful, as if she had begun to side with John against the idea.

'Do you have a job?'

'Looking,' he said brightly. 'A few things lined up. But I need a base, an address. Been in London a while, see. I'm from up here, but I've been away.'

'Well, we did say we were looking for someone in regular work.' She considered the panicky options of telling him that the room had been taken or that they had decided to let only to a woman.

'I can pay.' He looked hurt. 'Two, three weeks in advance.'

As he reached into his jeans pocket John came out of the lounge, his appearance at Myra's side making the man smile and relax.

'My husband,' said Myra. 'John.'

John leaned forward to shake hands, a gesture which seemed to amuse the man.

'Alex,' he said. 'Um, Harrison.'

'Well, come on, Myra, invite the man in. It's tipping down. Come inside, Alex.'

'Thanks.'

Myra reluctantly stepped aside, concerned about John's amiability which she knew to be forced.

The man, Alex, closed the door himself, dropping his bag by the coat rack, brushing droplets of rain from the waxy sleeves of his coat.

'Bloody weather. England, eh? Soon be winter too,' he said.

Myra caught a whiff of beer on his breath.

'Will you show him round, Myra?' said John. 'Or shall I?'

Myra saw this offer as a challenge to her resolve over the whole matter, a dare compounded by his pointed smile. He did not wait for an answer, touching her arm and going down the hall to the kitchen. Alex appeared unaware of this small tension, looking about the hallway, nodding appreciatively as he unbuttoned his coat.

'Come with me,' said Myra, coolly. 'I'll show you upstairs first.'

'Thanks.'

He followed her up to the first and main landing, talking behind her shoulder.

'Great, these old terraced places. Fetch a bomb in London, at least before the property crash. Still, good value up here. Good family homes. Who'd have a semi, eh? Georgian, would it be?'

'No. About 1880, we think.'

She led him along the landing, half hoping he would notice the dullness of the paintwork, a damp stain beneath the window. At the furthest door she stopped.

'This would be yours.'

Myra entered first, switching on the bedside lamp, a move keenly rehearsed two weeks ago, but which she now went through perfunctorily. Alex looked at the old teak tallboy, opening its mirror door, fingering the brass handle. He glanced about the rest of the room, at the three-quarter bed, the cane chair, the chest of drawers Myra had lined with leftover wallpaper, the old brown carpet scuffed with hoover swipes.

'Good,' he said. 'Neat. Just the ticket, if you'll have me.'

Myra hesitated, looking to reverse the momentum, seeking the kind of words she would use to rebuff a salesman's pitch. She crossed in front of him and touched the turned-off radiator, shivering deliberately.

'As I said, we were looking for someone with a job. You have to be careful these days, I'm sure you'll understand.'

'Course I do. World's full of rogues. No need to tell me that.'

He went over to the window and looked out at the darkened playing field and the necklace of orange street lights beyond. Then he turned, eyeing the room again with a look of impatience, as if he had already made his mind up that he was staying.

'What kind of work do you do?' Myra asked, wanting more time, yet knowing that the longer the delay, the more difficult it would be to disappoint him.

'Turn my hand to anything. Not proud, me. I'd be looking first thing in the morning. And anyway, like I said, I can offer up front if it'll make you feel easier.'

He sniffed and pulled a ball of crushed notes from his pocket, holding it demurely in his big hand, nodding as he counted the denominations of tens and twenties.

'Here. Ninety. And another fifty. Extra half-week to show willing. If I don't pay after that you can always chuck me out again.'

Myra looked down at the money, folded, half concealed, offered like a tip to a hotel porter, the currency seeming suspect, belonging to the alien culture of boarding houses, a world of rootlessness and fluid morals that Myra had not properly imagined until now. Then she heard John coming up the stairs and through the door behind her.

'Everything to your liking then, Alex? Oh, and money already. That's good,' he said.

He went over to the radiator and turned it on, feeling the pipe for the arrival of warmth.

'It'll be all right in an hour or so, Alex. Warm as toast. You'll be OK in here tonight, won't he, love?' he said, winking at Myra before breezing back out of the room and down the stairs.

'Great. Well, here then.' He pushed the money towards her, wanting rid of it, the contract made binding.

Myra breathed in deeply and took the warm notes.

'I'll show you the rest of the house,' she said. 'We'll be having dinner soon.'

For an hour they sat at the table in the big back kitchen, picking their way through a risotto – half an idle afternoon in the making – to which Myra had now hurriedly added extra salad and sweetcorn to make it go round.

The conversation came fitfully to all three, Myra trying to remember the things she should be saying, telling Alex where he could leave his washing, advising him about the back door that needed a kick to close it, the dustbin they kept in the yard outhouse. The young man crouched over his food, nodding. 'Right. Thanks.' But he seemed unconcerned about such details and, when he could, in his increasingly revealed Yorkshire accent, he tried to divert the talk with unrelated comments about his having been born in Leeds, about football, about the red enamel lampshade over the table. John, polite and light-hearted, trailed after each remark with words of his own but his offerings were inapt, halting Alex's flow, leaving John to fill the silences with weak information about the shops on the top road and where Alex might find the nearest bank. This last comment drew a laugh from Alex and he seemed about to own up that he did not have a bank account, until he checked himself, letting the laughter become confused with a forced cough.

'Oh, and there's one other thing,' said John.

'What's that?' He was chasing the last morsels of food round the plate with his fork.

'We have one more guest, for the time being.'

'Get to meet him tonight, will I? Or is it a she?' he said, looking up with interest.

'You might meet him tonight,' said John, grinning.

Myra looked at him, his face forward in the light from above the table. He had not mentioned their supposed rodent interloper for over a week. And she still didn't believe him.

'John thinks we may have a mouse,' she said. 'Though he's the only one who's seen it so far.'

'It's true!' John protested. 'It exists. Really. It's probably somewhere in here right now, watching us. We should think of a name for him, assuming, of course, that it's a boy. I wonder if you can tell the difference just by looking at them?'

'Mickey,' said Alex.

'What?'

'Mickey Mouse.'

'Yes, of course,' said John with a laugh. 'Mickey.'

'So there'll be the four of us then?' said Alex, looking pleased to have amused John.

'The four,' said John.

'Cosy.'

'Yes, Alex. Cosy.'

'You've no kids then?'

'No,' said John.

Myra looked quietly away.

When he had finished eating Alex sat back with a stifled burp, rubbing the puppy paunch beneath his shirt.

'Look at the size of that,' he said, looking down at the folds of flesh he was holding in his hands. 'Still, lovely meal. Thanks. Fond of Italian, me.'

'Yes, Myra,' said John, staring hard, quizzically at their guest. 'That was nice. You'll do well for food here, Alex.'

'Not that big an eater, really. The odd binge now and again, you know, out on the town.'

'Yes.' John sat back, his curiosity suddenly thinning. 'Well, if you'll forgive me I think I may call it a day. Work tomorrow, Alex. Sorry and all that. Myra will look after you, won't you, darling?'

'No fuss needed,' said Alex, meshing and cracking his fingers in front of him.

'Yes. Well, right,' said John.

Myra frowned at him, not wanting to be left alone with the stranger. But John avoided her look, kissed her and left the room.

When he had gone Alex sat forward, spinning a napkin ring on his finger until it fell into the clutter on the table. He looked at where it lay, not bothering to retrieve it.

'He's all right, isn't he? Your old man?'

'Yes,' said Myra. 'He's all right.'

'I should help clear this lot up,' he said, nodding at the dishes. 'Best start as we mean to go on. Good around the house, me. I'll do my share, don't you worry.'

'It doesn't matter. I often leave it till morning. Maybe you'd like to watch television for a while?'

'I'm not a fan.'

'A beer, then?'

'No.'

He was emphatic with this word, as if trying to create the impression of an unlikely abstemiousness.

Myra led him into the lounge anyway and he remarked approvingly about the real fire, seating himself in a deep armchair. Outside the wind boomed in the quiet street and a sweep of rain flailed the window.

'You've brought the storms with you,' said Myra, standing in front of the fire, staring at the closed curtains.

'Seems I have.'

'Did you come up today? From London?'

'I certainly did.'

'Which part?'

'Islington. Went there after King's Cross. Bit of a shithole, that place. D'you know London?'

'Not well. I haven't been for years.'

'You should make the effort. Get yourself down there. A world centre, London is.'

A world centre.

Myra went to the sideboard and took a packet of Silk Cut from the drawer.

'We were going to have a non-smoker. For the room, I mean. But we didn't know if one would want us,' she waved an unlit cigarette in the air. 'I like one now and then. John started again recently too. But he's more restrained than me. Have one?'

'Thanks.'

Myra offered him a light and he drew deeply, the way hardened smokers do with mild cigarettes.

'Good,' he said, rubbing smoke out of his eyes, drawing heftily again. 'Shouldn't really, should we? Smoke, I mean. Still, life'd be dull without a few vices, eh?'

Myra nodded, relaxed by the first rush of nicotine in her blood. Then she caught him staring at her, inspecting his landlady, the few grey hairs perhaps, or her height, or the way her skirt hung from her hips, or her small breasts. Myra drew on her cigarette and rubbed at her wedding ring. Anxious to fill the silence, she looked about the room at the chrome-framed landscapes on the anaglypta walls, at the cottage-style sofa, the old bookcase brimming with modern titles, the pot-pourri in a clam shell on the cracked mantelpiece – their possessions, hers and John's, mingling with the dowdier trappings that belonged to John's father in this, the house of John's father. This last point was not one she felt obliged to explain to Alex so instead she tried to remember the little stories that were attached to their things: the finding of the shell on a Welsh beach, the latest book she was reading. It was the sort of talk she had imagined having with a lodger on the first night, and it dawned on her now that she had always supposed that anyone they might take in would be a professional sort – a nurse, a law student, certainly a woman. What had she been thinking about?

With nothing said by either of them, Alex looked away, squinting at his cigarette, biting a bit of quick from his thumbnail. Then he stretched and yawned loudly, tossing the cigarette into the fire.

'Maybe I should get off,' he said. 'Been a long day. The travelling and that. You don't think about it till it gets to you.'

'Wait,' said Myra, putting out her cigarette. 'I'll turn the bed back for you. It needs a little airing. Five minutes, that's all.'

'That's all right by me.'

Myra left the room in relief, picking up the heavy bag that was still in the hall and taking it upstairs.

In the room the bedside lamp was still on, illuminating the staged look of the place, a readiness of her own making that made Myra feel gauche. She turned back the duvet and smoothed the bottom sheet. It didn't really need doing. She had come up here for some obscure, nervous reason, perhaps to claim proprietorial rights over the room for the last moments before the intruder took up residence.

The intruder? Why was she thinking of him that way? She went to their own bedroom to tell John that their guest was coming to bed, only to find him sound asleep. Then she returned downstairs to find Alex on the sofa, also asleep. He looked smaller lying down, younger still than the twenty-two or three she had taken him for. She looked at his face, its London pallor, the sleeping expression a little handsome, a little thoughtless. She imagined him holidaying in Marbella, a lager lout, made in England. Still, he was some mother's son, she thought, before putting the guard around the fire and fetching a blanket from the understairs cupboard. She draped the blanket carefully about his shoulders, turned off the light and quietly closed the door.

In the bedroom she undressed in the dark and got into bed, lying awake a while. Outside, the rains had stopped. She listened to the sound of a distant train and a car which came sploshing through the puddles in the street and stopped outside the house, its engine running as the occupants exchanged joky goodbyes with their friends before it reversed fifty yards to an alley where it turned round and went away. In near sleep the logic that had led Myra to this night began to return. Perhaps, she thought, it would not turn out so badly. It was something for her to do, a challenge of sorts, not too demanding. In the room downstairs she heard Alex give a single interrupted snore that made her want to giggle. Then, as sleep beckoned, John stirred beside her. He sat up in one startling movement.

'When there's time.' His voice was booming, unfamiliar, filling the room. 'Not now. Wrong time.'

Myra knew not to touch him or say anything. He half turned, making to get out of bed, pulling the covers from her. Then he was properly awake, leaning over Myra, his eyes visible and troubled in the weak light. Beads of sweat collected and ran in a rivulet across his forehead. Myra could feel the heat of his skin. He let out a soft breath, shook his head and apologised in his normal voice. Sighing heavily, he lay back and closed his eyes. He was asleep again within a minute.

'God, I thought I'd finished with that business,' said John.

'What business?'

'You know, last night. The bad dreams. What did I say?'

'Nothing. Don't think about it.'

He lay back on the pillow and closed his eyes, licking his lips with the tip of his tongue. 'Mmm. Maybe you're right.'

Myra too thought those times had passed – the late nights waking drenched in sweat, the calling out, never too sinister, but once persistent and troubling for John. It had been four months since the last one, she reckoned. She used to try and get him to talk about them, but he would only mumble that they were all pretty much the same: some patriarchal figure like his boss or a teacher from his old school reprimanding him for not eating his meals, for stealing, for eavesdropping on some important discussion. This would be followed by the classic scene of pursuit, of always being late for an appointment and never quite managing to get there. And was there anyone else in the dreams? No. Myra wondered if last night's recurrence was due to Alex's arrival, the way it might have thrown John's sense of security, stretching the thread that existed between mind and home, the fragile link people spoke of being broken when they'd had their houses burgled.

John opened his eyes again. His skin had that post-sleep yellowness and a flash of downy hair was matted to his forehead. He screwed his eyes shut then forced them wide open, propping himself up on his elbows and frowning at the clock at his side of the bed.

'Christ, half-past eight. Sir will not be pleased.'

'You owe them nothing,' said Myra, yawning. 'Think of all the weekends you put in.'

'True. I suppose if I'm half an hour late it might as well be an hour.'

He got out of bed and began dressing, slowly at first, then succumbing to the urge to catch up with lost time, dancing into his trousers, getting into a fluster over the finding of clean socks. Myra stayed in bed, out of his way, listening as he went to the bathroom, to the brushes and spits as he cleaned his teeth, the tap of his razor on the sink, the flushing of the toilet. She had not told him Alex was in the lounge and when he went downstairs she heard the mingling of male voices, John muttering an apology to which Alex responded with a grunt.

A few minutes later Myra stirred herself and went downstairs. John was already on his way out. He nodded towards the door of the lounge, holding a finger to his lips. 'Sssh. Baby's still asleep. See you tonight,' he whispered, giving Myra a kiss before he left.

Myra went to the kitchen and had her usual breakfast of a few spoonfuls of cereal and black coffee, a diet scarcely changed in her entire adult life. Once, when there had been work to face, it might have been followed by a cigarette or two, and she still felt the urge now, but she resisted it. She sided the clutter of last night's meal and passed back along the hall, pausing outside the lounge door, listening for Alex's breathing.

Hearing nothing she went upstairs to dress before going out herself.

The sky was bright, the clouds fat and creamy, and the streets had that recently vacated look, the morning rush of traffic having already crammed itself along Bootham and into the city centre. Myra, when she could afford the time, which had been on most days lately, would often idle away mornings like this, disdaining the use of her car, buying individual items of food from a few small shops she had come to know, walking as far as the art gallery, round the edge of town and back by the river. But today was different and she felt a gratifying sense of purpose in going to the supermarket and buying extra bread, milk, meat, imagining Alex to have a young man's powerful and constant appetite. At the check-out she deliberately paid with some of the notes he had given her, calculating what might be left to term profit. Then it clicked that this might actually be worthwhile, that she was working again, making out in life, and even in this small way it made her feel a part of the society she saw around her – the woman tethering her dog outside the store, a postman on his rounds, men from the water board repairing a burst main. Some unnamable reminder came to her from the distant past, her childhood perhaps, a vague joy arriving on the cool light air, making a rent in the veil that had clouded her perceptions for so long. A tiny page of new history was being written, and the town – at least the section of the city wall she could see across the road between an antiques shop and Bart's Bistro – seemed to be welcoming her, to be alive at last. It was a different town altogether. It was for her, favouring her, this new York.

This elation was still with Myra as she reached the top of their street and she could see all the way down the long gabled terrace. Now the house had a function, it served them, Myra and John. Until today it had always felt as if the place merely contained them, cool and alone, a brick manifestation of John's glass bubble. But that may have been due to the fact that it still belonged to Bill, John's father. He had bought the house, the biggest he could find, when he and John's mother had moved here from Manchester fifteen years ago. They had visited the town often and fallen in love with it. And when John had left home it must have seemed a reasonable idea. The house was to have been an investment for their old age. But John's mother had died, and as for Bill it was an investment that would now yield him no useful dividend . . .

When Myra opened the front door Alex stirred in the lounge. She went through to the kitchen and began putting the groceries away. Alex followed a few seconds later, looking older in the daylight, ravaged, as if he had been more under the influence of drink than he had seemed the night before.

'Sorry,' he said, with a heavy yawn and a leonine shake of the head. 'Last night, I mean. I'll make sure I sleep in the right place tonight. No problem.'

'Don't let it worry you. Coffee?'

'Thanks.'

His shirt was open and his feet were bare, a slovenliness that Myra thought deliberate, notice of his tenancy. He seated himself at the table, scratching his head. Feeling more relaxed in the light of morning, Myra resurrected an aspect of the previous evening's conversation, asking, as she had been shy to ask before, exactly why he had left London.

'Things are quiet down there,' he said. 'Bad really. You're the better-off relations up here these days. No kidding.'

'What was your work?'

'Did the markets. Second-hand clothes was the main thing, specially seventies stuff. Big now. But we'd sell anything – videos, records, bits of furniture, anything that could be moved. Then this guy, my partner, cleared off with the stock. One thing led to another . . . And here I am. Maybe I'd just had enough of the place. Maybe the noise, you know. And you can't trust anybody down there. Nobody.'

Myra listened attentively, detecting some truth in what he was saying, but feeling it to be the wrong shape, that some bigger story lay behind it, like trouble with the police, or a jilted pregnant girlfriend.

Alex went back into the lounge and returned with a Golden Virginia tin from which he rolled a cigarette. He lit it and sat back, tapping the handle of the coffee mug with his thumbnail.

'You've not had a lodger before then, Myra?'

It was the first time he had called her by her name, and its use seemed calculated.

'Actually, no,' Myra conceded. 'It's a new thing for us. It's such a big house. So many rooms. And John's at work all day, so we thought why not.'

'Thought so. Thought it was new for you. D'you not work yourself then, Myra?'

Now he was practising with the name, trying it for ease of use, its weight in the mouth.

'Yes. Well, I'm a supply teacher. There's not much going at the moment.'

'Shame,' he said, absorbed with the making of a number of cigarettes which he laid carefully in the tin.

Myra carried on putting the shopping in the cupboards and larder knowing, as he did not, the place for everything. It was her quiet way of repelling his territorial advances. But she did offer lunch, despite its not being part of the financial arrangements, the details of which they had yet to discuss fully.

'No,' he said. 'Things on today. But thanks.'
Thanks. The way he said that. Emptily.

In the afternoon Alex went out and for once Myra welcomed having the house to herself. For all that she had complained to John about the loneliness of such times, today it was a relief to claim sole occupancy, to cast herself unchallenged into the space in each empty room.

She had often cautioned herself against spending too much time alone, remembering Stella, a cousin who had lapsed into a brief state of paranoia which Myra's mother had insisted was because Stella had married young, had children, and had given up on the idea of engaging with the world on any other level. If that was the real reason, Myra thought, such an infliction would never come her mother's way. No secret compartments waiting to burst open in her. She was sixty-five now and loving every minute of it, her vital ways still intact, scouring Southport dance clubs, upsetting amateur dramatic societies, always on the look-out for a boyfriend. On the hunt, she would say mischievously, paling the expressions of less game lady friends a decade younger than her. And why not, Myra would think, proud of her mother, knowing the cheap fate that old age had in store for some. Like Bill.

Poor Bill. Myra sometimes used afternoons like this to clear more of Bill's things away to the attic. If John ever noticed their disappearance he never mentioned it, though he was concerned about their doing too much decorating – his sister Connie might object to their getting too comfortable in the house that would be half hers when Bill died. Myra knew Connie and did not think she would find her wish to change a few things unreasonable, though she kept them to a minimum, insisting only on painting the lounge and kitchen, and in shades close to the originals. It was then that she found bits of paper stuck behind pictures on the walls, in cracks in the bare plaster in a cupboard. They were written in an infantile hand, fragmentary and repetitive shopping lists, meaningless sentences and reminders about unexplained dates, sad chronicles of Bill's journey into silence, a silence that gave back none of its hostages. She told John nothing of her discoveries, agonising about throwing the scraps away, eventually deciding to bury them deep among Bill's belongings in the two upper rooms.

Today she decided only to tidy the lounge. Afterwards, as was her habit, she lifted the sash window a few inches so that she could hear the sounds of people in the street, then she settled guilt-free in front of the television. Anyone who despised television was a fool, she thought. It was the perfect panacea – company for the elderly, soothing the dissolute, the socially ungifted, subtle as nicotine. It put the dampers on conscious thought, drawing away the jabbering edges of wakeful time. Torrid news, soap operas – the feebler, the better – the transport of delight that came with the violin accompaniment to an advert for margarine, it was all there in that box in the corner, the box of surprises that could be opened and turned off at will. It was a recent thing with Myra, but nowadays she could watch anything and be shamelessly engaged. The telly. It afforded . . . relief.

That afternoon Myra caught the last ten minutes of a new and wonderfully tacky game show followed by the whole of a 1947 black and white film. This, a romantic comedy set in Ireland, held her attention fully. Something about the monochrome scenery moved her, seduced her into thinking it more real than life itself. The characters' lives were so untrammelled, paradigms of perfect logic. And there was the cottage by the silver lake, the endless sunshine, the moral codes that ruled the villagers' lives – this last aspect something to which Myra, with memories of her own, attached no significance. When the ending came, perfectly predictable and satisfying, a garish trailer for children's TV appeared and Myra hurried to turn the set off, hoping to preserve her tranquil reception of the film for a little while longer. At least until John came home. Or Alex.

John arrived first, at six thirty. He kissed her and she smelt the sweat of the office on his shirt, a life of work, duty, habit. A good life. Blameless, if he would but believe it. She followed him through to the kitchen where he opened his case and waved a folded paper bag, grinning.

'For our guest. The non-paying one.'

'Pardon?'

'The mouse. The damned mouse. I swear to God we have one. I saw it again the other day. You should see the little bugger move. Haven't you at least heard it scratching about?'

'No, I haven't.'

'Well, I'll catch it and then you'll believe me.'

'I never said I didn't believe you.'

'Mmm.' He was puzzling over the wire mechanism. He put the trap on the draining board and teased it with a knife, springing back when it snapped shut. He laughed.

'Well, that should do it. A bit of bacon rind on the spike, not cheese, mind you, and . . .' He set it again. 'One ex-mouse. Deceased. No longer to be.'

He put the trap behind a box on the pantry floor and returned, rubbing his hands.

'So, how's it been? With our other house friend, Alex?'

'Seems all right. Friendly enough. A bit of a rogue maybe, underneath it all. As long as he pays, I suppose . . .'

'And keeps his hands off the family silver.'

'Yes, that.'

'I wonder if he plays chess. Maybe he'd like to learn.'

John took off his jacket and went to the sink to wash his hands. 'You haven't said anything to him, have you?'

'About what? Chess?'

'No. You know, about us.'

'I told him what I do for a living, when I can. I asked him a bit more about himself. What else am I supposed to have said?'

'Well, you know . . .'

Myra sighed.

'We're meant to be putting all that behind us.'

'It was just a thought, since the fellow's going to be part of the family. Perhaps we should explain more about ourselves. It would seem only fair, only honest for us to . . . own up.' He turned to face her, one eyebrow raised with that cool challenging look of his that Myra hated.

'It would be pointless, and you know it. There's nothing to own up to, nothing to be ashamed of . . .'

'Of course, sorry.' He held up his wet hands in mock surrender with a sour smile that was worse than the earlier expression. 'Sorry, sorry, sorry. Only . . .'

'Only nothing. John – '

But she was interrupted by the banging of the front door.

'So, so,' said Alex, shambling into the kitchen. 'What's for dinner? Starving, me. Or is it too early?'

'Certainly not, Alex,' John said, brightly. 'It's not too early, is it, Myra?'

Myra looked at her husband, annoyed by the unfinished business of their conversation.

'No,' she said. 'I'm going to start it now.'

4

The village they moved to, eighteen months ago, was called Little Pawnton. There had been a Great Pawnton, but all that remained of that now was the black cross of antiquity on an OS map. It was not too far out and at night, if the clouds were low, they could still see the lights of Manchester reflected in the sky. But it was a very different world, a village neither pretty nor mundane, facing east towards the bare-knuckled horizon of the moors with its dry-stone walls and barns, the limestone runnels where ragged sheep wet their tongues. To the west was farmland with pot-holed roads cut deep beneath the fields. In the village itself there was a Norman church, two pubs, one shop, a closed-down school up for sale, a stream running cold and clear beneath a stone bridge, and on the main approach a tiny Heritage Centre had been built with a tarmac car-park for the coaches and cars that brought the ramblers. It was averagely charming, usual, like a dozen other villages in the area, though that spring, Myra had to admit, the hills looked almost too beautiful to bear. And like all the other villages Pawnton had been half colonised by people like Myra and John, refugees from the city. The locals could hardly afford to live there any more, their young often making the reverse journey to find homes and work in Manchester and other Lancashire towns. It was an old story, and those that could stay in the village afforded a grudging tolerance to the newcomers, humouring them, accusing them, Myra was once to hear, of throwing mud on their Range Rovers to give them rural authenticity.

Their new home was the last of a row of five former tied cottages, two streets removed from the main street and the most southerly house in the village. And like most of the houses it had been treated to the full gauntlet of 'modernisation' with central heating, triple glazing, wall insulation, all the building know-how that could be mustered in defiance of the harsh moorland winters. Behind the house was a long garden bordered by a stone wall, a stunted chestnut tree in one corner which, after standing there for half a century, blew down in the first gale they encountered, four days after moving in. It lay there a long time amidst the sprawling weeds of a piece of land Myra felt they were unwise to have taken on. But each morning Myra went out there just to breathe the air, to dine on its sweetness and give thanks for their arrival which they quickly agreed had been the right thing, for all their sakes – Myra's and John's. And Laura's . . .

'Mrs Wentworth?'

The sound of her own surname surprised Myra. She hadn't heard it spoken aloud in a long time. It sounded like it was being read from one of her cheques or a misdirected letter.

'Yes?'

'My name's Rowena Knapton. I'm headmistress of Bow-handy Without. Your name's on the supply list.'

The list. She was indeed reading from a list.

'Oh, right.'

'Well, I'm after help. Five mornings a week. Straight away, if you're interested. It'll probably be till the end of term.'

'I see.' She leaned against the hall wall, pressing down a bubble in a seam of the wallpaper with her finger. 'To be honest, I'd rather forgotten l was on the list. I've not worked for a while. I could be terribly rusty. Would that matter?'

A fifty-fifty chance. Either it should matter or the caller had already made up her mind to gamble with a new face, perhaps giving undue attention to some detail on Myra's quite ordinary CV.

'Not to me, love.'

Love. This was Yorkshire.

'So, fancy it?'

'Well, yes,' said Myra, trying to hide her reluctance, knowing that a refusal might make this the last offer she would receive.

'Tomorrow?'

'Right. Why not?'

'Good. I'll see you then. Myra, isn't it?'

'It is.'

Myra put the phone down. She had hoped to keep teaching as an option she might pursue more vigorously next year if her other ideas dried up – those possibilities which all came to mind in that moment: her vague plans for training in hotel management, or nursing, or the rather obvious computer studies that were suitable for a woman of her background. But she had done so little about them, countering each idea with excuses for putting it aside until a more appropriate time, all the result, Myra believed, of an unforgivable lassitude.

Afterwards she was glad she had agreed to take the job – it would have been perverse to refuse. Perhaps she needed to be told what to do, perhaps she was that kind of an animal. And if nothing else, it might add further impetus to the livelier existence she was seeking. John should be pleased and Alex, after five days, had not been half the burden she expected. He spent the day out, he never said where, going out again in the evenings. Over the weekend he had left the house on Saturday morning and not returned until late on Sunday night. 'Visiting mates,' he explained voluntarily. Myra did not mention the wasted Saturday evening meal, deciding not to start making dinner until she knew he was in the house, not bothering with him at all if he was not around before nine o'clock. She knew she should clarify the arrangement with him, but for now the modesty of his demands could be useful to her and she was reluctant to apply any formal restraints to their growing relationship.

John, working long hours on an urgent tender for a warehouse in Leeds, seemed relaxed about Alex's presence, accepting him like a wayward relative, even taking sides with him against Myra in their joky conversations at dinner. On that first weekend Myra had found him in Alex's room, laughing and shaking his head at the clutter, the coffee jar lid he was using as an ashtray, the cellophane packet of razors on the window sill, clothes spilling from the still half-full holdall. As Myra brushed past him to open the window he said, 'What a pit! The old man would have kittens. Still, he's not so bad, is he? Our Alex?' And on the evening Myra told him about the job offer, his first reaction was, 'What about the boy? He'll be home alone. How will he manage?' And he laughed.

The next morning Myra drove out to Bowhandy. She had not used her car for weeks, preferring to walk wherever she could, both by way of exercise and for the time it took up in her eventless days. Thus the red Metro had been standing in the street outside the house like a sulky waiting dog, attracting quaintnesses in its grime such as 'LUFC' and 'Fuck you'.

The day was breezy and dull, this bit of England dry

under the blanket of grey Myra had seen on last night's BBC weather map. In the streets older children were fooling around on their way to school, contemplating truancy perhaps, while shop and office workers skipped around them, heading for town in quiet contained moods. When Myra reached the lights at Clifton Green she felt a rush of anxiety about returning to work after so long away from the job. She began to worry that the sweatshirt she was wearing might be too informal, but it was too late to turn back. She had not taught full-time for over two years – her nominal spell of work round here hardly seeming to count. That had been across town, a political appointment, she soon found out, a contrivance to jolt the holder of the permanent post into not taking so much time off with 'stress'. And it did the trick, the woman marching back into the school days before her latest sick note ran out, announcing her arrival to no one, barging into Myra's classroom and taking over, tearful but determined.

Myra had seen Bowhandy before, on her way with John to a shopping complex on that side of town. It was in the middle of a housing estate, a single new building of pink brick and glass, the doors picked out in scarlet and grey. Beyond it the horizon consisted of unfinished roofs with glimpses in between of the farmland and trees retreating from the bulldozers' advances. But it pleased Myra – it would be a change from the kind of Victorian pile she had known in Manchester. Here she might find that air of optimism that went with newness, a freedom from the obligations of history that would suit her frame of mind perfectly.

Rain began falling in heavy spits as she drove into the car-park. The only other person in sight was a woman running to the main double doors. She waited, holding one door open with her foot as Myra got out and ran across the playground. By the time she reached the school the rain had stopped and sunshine instantly and unbelievably flooded the area.

'Rowena,' said the woman.

She was stocky, about forty-five with short greying hair, heavy black-rimmed glasses, a thick roll-neck sweater and tweed skirt. In her arms was a dissembling heap of folders and papers from beneath which she extended her hand. They went inside and the headmistress pointed out a few features of the building.

'Thermostatically controlled roof windows. Not so bad. Last place I worked at, the heating was controlled at the town hall seven miles away.' She led the way to her office. 'The nerve centre,' she said, dropping her burden on another pile of papers stacked in an armchair. 'Or nervous breakdown centre, if you like.'

'That bad, is it?' Myra took off her coat, exposing the yellow sweatshirt. Rowena looked at her. Domesticated, thought Myra, she thinks I'm the little housewife, an amateur.

'No. You'll like it here.'

Rowena yawned, took off her glasses and looked in a mirror on the filing cabinet behind her desk. She put her glasses back on and stared dully out of the window at the parents' cars arriving in the car-park.

'They only live across the road. You'd think they could walk that bit, wouldn't you?'

Myra said nothing, her apprehension about being here returning with a stab as she heard the children's voices and saw the tops of their heads flitting past the window.

'We've five minutes yet,' said Rowena. 'I suppose I should fill you in on a few things. You're here for Georgina, a full-timer who's just discovered she's seven months pregnant. Can you believe it? Anyway, they'd only let me take someone on half-time and I had to fight for that. Truth is, we've had a bit of a problem justifying our existence. Only half the intake we expected. There just aren't the kids. Most of the ones we've got come from the estate there. Legoland. We've a few travellers' kids too. The authentic article though, no didicoys.' She scratched behind her ear, looking at the desk as if searching for the way she was meant to start the day. 'They're all right, the gypsies. One of them left last week and I had the father in here, thanking me for looking after his daughter. You don't get that too often. The syllabus, by the way, includes the latest state assessment thing. Any ideas on that?'

'I haven't had much to do with it, I'm afraid. I'll need to read up on it.'

'Well, Myra, when you've worked it out, let us know. We're not so sure ourselves.'

Myra smiled, but it was only to mask an anxiety that was being fuelled by the cries and running feet in the corridor. She felt faint, claustrophobic, as if this room, the whole building, was holding her prisoner. It was a passing from the solitude she had known for so long back to life lived by someone else's rules. She was mixing it with the world of people again and, momentarily, she felt nostalgic for her old indolent existence. Then a small young woman with tangled ginger hair flounced into the office.

'Kate,' said Rowena. 'This is Myra. The cavalry.'

The woman, Kate, tossed her bag on to the filing cabinet and dropped her coat on top of the papers in the armchair.

'So, Myra,' she said. 'Here to help, are you?'

'Yes. I think that's the idea,' Myra said coolly.

'Well, if you've done this job before, you'll know the basic truth that nothing can be taught. It can only be offered. The little loves will take it if they want it. And if they don't . . . It's the modern way, I'm afraid.' She turned to the mirror to examine a small blemish on her freckled cheek. Myra, more composed now, wondered if she would end up going through the mirror routine each morning. It seemed required behaviour.

Rowena slipped from the room with Kate, when she noticed she had gone, flying after her.

'A word, Rowena, please,' she called. 'Now, if you don't mind.'

Myra breathed deeply, glad of a few seconds alone before she followed, trailing the other two at a distance, feeling more at home among the children gathering outside the hall, tumultuous and beautiful-skinned, their numbers hardly bothering to part for the headmistress who was shaking her head, waving away her colleague's apparently animated supplications.

Rowena helped out for the first hour, pointing out the grouping of the children according to their skills, showing Myra the Water Project that her predecessor had begun. And when she had gone, Myra's worries about returning to teaching began to fade. Old joys came back, the exercising of long-known, ineradicable skills. When the children became restless she simply clapped her hands and they sat obediently, though noses were picked, and there were the sniffs and splutters of autumn colds, an innocence in the expressions of some that made Myra's eyes prickle, a mischief in the hands and kicking feet of others that tempered her sensitivity. How could she have forgotten all this? This goodness?

At morning break she briefly met the other member of staff, Andrew, a young man who took the juniors and who seemed to want to keep himself to himself, a creature of habit, institutionalised perhaps, the way teachers could become. But Myra would not be judgemental, deciding to try and make her time among them as harmonious as possible, avoiding the creeping prejudices she had known afflict so many in the profession. Her profession, she thought with a sense of privilege.

That evening, at dinner, Myra reflected on her reawoken sense of the structure that employment lent to life. She was full of herself, but reticent, as if the satisfactions of the day were too fragile to risk in conversation. John and Alex were quiet too until, after he had finished eating, Alex sat back in his usual way, patting the pot stomach.

'Grand that. Thanks.'

'Aye, grand,' John said, grinning.

Myra kicked him under the table. He had said to her, in a recent résumé of Alex's habits, that he always sat back from the table and said exactly that. Alex though, if he suspected ridicule, said nothing. For the last hour his reserve had struck Myra as an attempt at good manners, as if he might be trying to refine his behaviour for their sakes. He smiled in a new and unnatural way, lips tight, head slightly bowed as he looked across the table at John.

'How's work then, John?' he asked.

'OK, Alex. Things look a bit dodgy now and then. But there's a recession on, everyone knows that.'

'Oh?'

'Trouble is, people tend to use it as an excuse, turning their backs on the job, forgetting how it's done. It's the great British malaise, I'm afraid. We're scared of recovery, success, scared of ideas.'

'Wasn't like that when Thatcher was around,' said Alex. 'She'd have sorted this mess out. They shouldn't have finished her off like they did. Criminal, that.'

John smiled tolerantly.

'Well . . . I don't know.'

Myra sat back, pleased not to be involved.

'Bit boring though, isn't it?' said Alex. 'Your job, I mean. Being stuck in an office all day.'

'Absolutely. Useless, really. But then what job isn't? I

read the other day that fifteen per cent of the working population could provide the lot of us with all we need – food, housing, energy. The rest of us are doing nothing more than making and moving material goods, or else just policing their distribution. Totally unnecessary, including the stuff I do. You see, Alex,' he said, hands rising as he warmed to his subject, 'we're too well off in the West. We've got nothing to do but invent our needs. And it makes us miserable. We deem ourselves intelligent, above the rest of the animal kingdom. And we feel obliged to force our sweet breathing selves into the boxes and grids of a linear existence. It's unnatural. And it hardly works anyway. That's why there's still crime, wars, why we have the capacity to hate each other. We're still beasts, really.'

'So it's back to the caves then, is it?' said Alex, with a snigger.

'No. It's not,' John said sharply, annoyed with Alex's obtuseness. 'I don't know what the answer is.'

'Better off not thinking about it at all,' said Myra.

'Sure,' said John, still vexed, his argument wasting on stony ground. 'You could go mad thinking about it, how pointless it all is.'

He sat back, deep in thought.

Myra had not heard this kind of talk from him for a while. It was the sort of thing he used to come out with in Manchester at the company promotion events he hated, where the men came to compare wives, to boast about their latest holidays. It was his means of having a dig at his colleagues, letting them know he had a brain that worked independently of the daily grinding system. It neither earned him respect nor made him unpopular. It was John. The way he was. A bit deep.

Alex pushed his chair back and stood, patting the change in his pockets.

'That's enough heavy talk for me,' he said. 'I think I'll be going out for an hour. I was thinking about that place down the road, The Flying Horse. Want to come?' The words hung on the air. 'It'd be a lark, eh? The three of us?'

He was staring at the space between his two hosts and Myra felt a flush of pity for him, his attempt at politeness and the vulnerability it revealed.

'Good of you to ask, Alex. But we're not really the pub sort these days, are we, Myra?'

'Well, I don't know . . .'

'And, frankly I'm a bit done in,' he said, nipping a bit of dirt from under his thumbnail. Thus he reveals a less elegant self, thought Myra, a conventional core beneath the dreamy philosophies. 'Mind, there's nothing stopping you, Myra, if you want to go.'

'I don't know . . .'

'Go. It'll do you good.' He smiled impishly. 'It'll help you unwind from the day's exertions.'

'I've got work tomorrow too, remember?' Myra said, struggling with her reserve, the same petty aloofness she had found so repellent in John just seconds before.

'Oh, come on. The fellow's waiting. Look.'

Alex was standing by the door with a look of impending triumph.

'Well, for an hour, I suppose . . .'

'Good. That's settled then. About time too,' said Alex. 'Meet you at the door in two minutes.'

He left the room. John chuckled.

'You could have made the effort,' said Myra. 'He's only trying to be friendly.'

'I know. That's what makes it so funny. Oh, l couldn't face it. You'll be all right, though. Maybe you'll get a game of darts or something.'

'Hah, bloody hah.'

'No, seriously. It might do you good, a young man's company. You might enjoy it.'

'What do you mean by that?'

'Nothing.'

A minute later Alex came clumping down the stairs and put his head round the door.

'You ready, Myra?'

'Aye, lad,' said John, grinning. 'Aye, she's ready.'

5

The pub, not two hundred yards from the house, was somewhere Myra had not been before. Alex led her into the bar, a smoky L-shaped room with mock carriage lamps and handwritten Day-Glo notices about quiz night, a pool tournament. High in one corner was a television to which no one was paying attention, its babble smothered by the jukebox. And mingling with the cigarette smoke was a smell of microwaved pizza.

While Myra sat down a man approached Alex, nodding towards the pool table near the toilet doors. Alex gestured towards Myra with a backward nod, then came over to ask if she minded him playing pool for ten minutes. Myra said it was fine by her. She sat back with her drink, content to watch.

Further down the long wall seat Myra had chosen were two young women, daughters of the town, she presumed, the only other women in the room. They lit cigarettes, talking and laughing, glancing occasionally at the bar and the pool table. Myra felt a pleasurable sense of camaraderie with them, a sisterhood afforded by their mutual exclusion from the concerns of the men. She wondered about their habits, their loves, the places they might go to of an evening, feeling a pulse of envy for what she assumed to be the simplicity of their lives. Then, when one of them commented that Myra was staring at them, her sympathies changed. She looked back towards the pool table.

She knew nothing about the game, but watched attentively as Alex bent over the table, his jumper lifting to reveal a loop he had missed in threading the belt through his jeans. He held the cue with a light, almost feminine grip, his shots thoughtfully weighted in contrast to his opponent's frustrated swipes. They had to share the only cue there was, the other man reluctantly giving up his possession of it each time he missed a pot. When Alex had to play an intricate shot he drew admiring comments from three men standing at the bar. Friends of his, it seemed, already more friends than she and John had made in all their time in York. Alex won the game despite a late hasty effort from his opponent. When the two men turned away into the corner and money was handed over, Myra looked away, mildly embarrassed. Then Alex joined her. She complimented him on winning.

'You've played before,' she said.

'Not much. Not really. Kids' stuff, pool. Snooker's my game. Played a lot in London, in the clubs. Won a couple of tournaments.'

'Really?'

'Local stuff.' He shrugged. 'Nothing special.'

'You should keep it up. It might get you somewhere.'

'Doubt it.' He licked the paper of the cigarette he was rolling. 'The top guys, the pros, they're just too good. They've got it all sewn up between them. No room for the likes of me. Too old already.'

Myra resisted the urge to ask him just what his age was, thinking he might tell her a lie.

'By the way,' he said, lighting the cigarette, spitting a fleck of tobacco from his lip. 'Your old man, John. He wasn't taking the piss out of me back there, was he?'

'No,' said Myra. 'Of course not.'

Alex turned to face her, propping his elbow against the back of the seat.

'See, when I make a joke, right, when he laughs, it's as if he's laughing at me and not the joke.'

'That's not the case, Alex, honestly. It's just his way of, well, letting his hair down. He likes you, really he does. It's just that sometimes he's a bit tense. He finds it hard to let his real feelings show.'

'Mmm.'

'If you thought he was being nasty, it's a mistake.' Myra felt her cheeks reddening. 'It's not meant that way, believe me.'

'That's all right then.' He turned to watch the new game in progress at the pool table.

He went quiet, sipping little and often at his beer as if unsatisfied with Myra's explanation. And indeed his remark about John had thrown her, laying bare their conceited belief that Alex suspected nothing unusual about their household. Myra's mind filled with ways of fielding a defence of John, and she struggled with the idea of blurting out the real reason for their coming to York.

'It's to do with lots of things. It's . . .' she began.

'It's what?' Alex said, but he was twitching, ghosting a shot that a man was playing at the table.

'Oh, it . . . doesn't matter.'

The silence stayed Myra's urge for confession and after a while she felt able to force some neutral conversation. She asked him how his search for work was progressing. He replied gruffly that he had been looking, but there wasn't much doing, officially, whatever that meant. Then he nodded in the direction of a fat, shaven-headed, middle-aged man who was standing at the bar doing a wobbling dance to a Max Bygraves song he had put on the juke-box for a laugh. His name, Alex said, was Terry. He had 'sidelines', which Myra took to mean he was 'officially' claiming the dole. One of these was carpet fitting which he did for a department store in town. He had told Alex he might be able to shuffle some work his way, if he wanted it.

'And I might,' said Alex. 'As a last resort. The old capital's drying up a bit. Prefer something permanent though. Then I could get fixed up with a flat of my own.'

Myra was cowed by this comment, thinking it retaliatory, a way of showing that he still felt stung by John's condescending attitude.

'You'll stay then? In York, I mean,' she said, with a coolness of her own.

He smiled, thawing sourly.

'Reckon so. I've had London. Had it. Nothing to me now, that place. Off the map as far as I'm concerned.'

Not for the first time, Myra was suspicious about this directness of his, a quality at once both honest and doubtful, a subservience to the senses that might be contradicted within an hour, a minute, according to his mood. But then he was young. It was permissible, she supposed.

They stayed another hour, Alex mellowing, stepping up his drinking tempo without caring what his landlady might think. Myra began to relax too, forgetting their small confrontation, the labours of the day and her fourth glass of wine inducing a pleasant weariness that she wanted to prolong until she was home, until sleep. And when time was called she rather regretted it, watching the men drift drunkenly happy from the room, their smoke left thinning in the air. Then she and Alex left too, walking home in the unexpected balminess of an Indian summer night.

Back at the house Myra went through to the kitchen. She felt a little tipsy, a little in love with herself, with the most trivial of things – the row of mugs on their hooks beneath a cupboard, the old white wall tiles and their filigree blue cracks. This was Bill's kitchen, it was her kitchen, either way it did not matter: ownership was a frame of mind, no more. And she loved her own hand as it lifted the kettle and held it under the tap. She must sober up, she thought. Then a touch on her shoulder stilled her euphoria. She turned to find Alex right behind her, smiling.

'What? What do you want?'

He leaned forward and kissed her high on the cheek.

'For tonight. It's been good.'

Myra's sense of well-being took a sideways shift. He squeezed her shoulders and rubbed his forehead against hers, the smell of beer and cigarettes on his breath. He lifted his mouth towards hers.

'No, Alex.'

She pressed him gently on the chest, concerned that he was too great a weight for her to move. But he backed away, surprisingly.

'Hey, sorry.' He held up his hands. 'No harm meant. Just testing the temperature. I wasn't . . .' He scratched his head, smiling to himself. 'Look, I'm sorry, Myra.'

'It's all right. Don't worry about it.'

'Friends?'

'Yes.'

He faked a yawn and half turned away.

'I reckon I should be off to bed.'

'Would you like a drink first?'

'Nah. Reckon I've had enough, don't you?'

The refrigerator clicked off, leaving total silence, a silence that was inviting Myra to make some comment, to bring her wisdom to bear on the moment.

'Wait,' she said.

His expression changed to one of boyish curiosity, the eyes concentrating, head tilted. Myra swallowed, unsure of herself, struggling with her slight drunkenness, the wish to make good, make light of the situation.

'Are you sure I can't get you anything?'

It was a foolish thing to say. A howler. She was confusing

him and his smile was now one of naïve triumphalism, bloke-ish, better placed in the bar they had just been in.

'Not tonight, Myra. But thanks anyway.' He took a step backwards. 'Next time, maybe. See you.'

'Goodnight, Alex.'

He turned, opening the door, hesitating with his broad back to her, before going out and up the stairs.

And when Myra heard him in the bathroom above her, peeing heavily, flushing the old box cistern that cranked up like the first notes of a bass overture, she wanted to laugh out loud, though for what reason, she did not know.

'He kissed you?'

'A peck. Here, actually.' Myra pointed to the spot high on her face. 'Navigational problem, I think. Nearly got my eye.' She didn't know why she was telling him. Nothing had happened, it was a non-incident, perfectly forgettable. Perhaps it was her thick throat, the post-drinking guilt that was giving her the urge to confess something.

John laughed.

'Maybe he has designs on you.'

'Oh, come on.' It had been a mistake to say anything. She should have kept quiet, or fobbed John off with some dismissive comment about the evening.

'Why shouldn't he? A red-blooded young male. You're an attractive woman, Myra.'

Was she? For the last few years her looks had been a side issue as far as she was concerned. If she bothered to linger by the bathroom mirror she might, on a poor day, notice the narrowness of the upper lip that gave her a mildly impudent look, or the distance between the soft brown eyes that denied her exceptional prettiness. And there were two fine lines descending from each corner of the mouth, a looseness of the skin under the eyes – thirty-something wrinkles that could be soothed by moisturiser but never revitalised. And her hair was always too long and uncertain in style. But the threads of white suited her. And on better days she would see that there was still youth in her face, would always be, her features set in tranquil reflection of the creature she was – resilient, optimistic.

'Positive thinking,' she said aloud. 'Worth more than looks any day.'

'Sorry?' John said, in earnest pursuit of books and papers, late for work again.

'Nothing. Just a thought.' She leaned out of the way as he struggled into his coat. 'Funny, Alex has never mentioned girlfriends. I wonder if he has one?' A successful comment, spontaneous. 'Maybe we should ask in case he wants to invite one back.'

'Hardly our business, I'd have thought.'

'No. Maybe not.'

John ducked into the pantry and she heard him slide the box on the stone floor to inspect the mousetrap. He backed out, looking disappointed.

'Last night, when you were out, I thought I heard something . . . Oh, never mind,' he said. 'By the way, this weekend . . .'

'Yes?'

'I thought we might go and see Dad. It's been a while.'

He straightened his collar slowly, staring down at some point at the other side of the room.

'If you like.'

'Yes.' He picked up his briefcase, gaze still fixed on the same place on the wall. 'Yes, I think it's time we went again.'

'All right.'

He kissed her and she watched him go down the hall, still shrugging himself into the coat that had always been a size too small for him. Attractive, she thought. He still thinks me attractive. Did she want to be told that, these days? Perhaps.

That morning, with the first hour and a half over, Myra joined the rest of the staff in the quiet room near the kitchen. Andrew was planted firmly behind the *Guardian*, Rowena was plumped awkwardly on one of the small classroom chairs and Kate, in puce Lycra leggings and sloppy joe jumper, was curled luxuriantly in the one armchair in the room, smiling at the ring on her finger.

'It's so real. It's just . . . there.' She turned the silver band with its small ruby stones. 'Bit slack maybe. I could get it tightened, I suppose. But that wouldn't be right somehow, considering David went to so much trouble. It would be quaint to leave it as it is, slightly imperfect. Don't you think?'

The remark fell short of any particular audience. Rowena touched her glasses and sipped coffee. If she was bored she was concealing it heroically.

'How long have you known him?' Myra asked politely.

'Two months now,' she said, the smile subduing, as if she wished one of the others were asking a more advanced question. 'Seems longer. Really.'

'And have you a date for getting married?'

Rowena stirred, recrossing her short legs.

'Bit of an old chestnut that one, isn't it, Katie?' she said.

'Not really. I don't see anything getting in my way this time.'

Andrew lowered his newspaper with a plain, dry look and Myra sensed the presence of an old ghost, a friction to which she was not yet privy.

'What does he do, this . . . David?' Andrew asked, emphatic with the name's consonants.

'He's a mechanic. At Billy Bright's on Hull Road,' said Kate, still looking at the ring.

'And where will you live? Your flat?'

'It's a possibility. Actually we've been thinking about buying a place of our own. David said we might look this weekend.'

'What about his mother?' asked Rowena.

'What about her? He only lives with her because it's cheap. That way he can save. Right?'

Rowena said nothing, staring blankly at the ring while Kate descended into a fit of giggling.

At a minute before half-past, Myra went to call the children in. Her head was still a bit woolly and it was a relief to get away from the others, to maintain the polite distance afforded to a newcomer. She also did not want to discuss her own life, though if asked she had all the answers neatly prepared. She had been married for seven years. John was an architect's deputy. They had moved from Manchester for his job. They lived in his father's house. They had taken in a lodger to make ends meet. Stock details, not perfectly true, but Myra knew she could deliver them confidently, unadorned, in a way that would inspire no deeper inquisition. They were childless, yes, but that was hardly rare these days, and few ever thought to pursue that line beyond asking if they had ever considered starting a family. To which she would answer . . . sometimes.

Standing at the school's side door, ringing the bell, Myra pushed the possibility of having to parry such a question out of her mind. For now, Myra was simply Myra, a grain of sand, a microbe in the big wide universe. Myra, a bit of a dull type really, thirty-seven, not unattractive, as John had kindly remarked. Given to boredom perhaps, even tetchiness, yet not a woman to have hidden depths. It was how she meant herself to be seen. Ordinariness personified.

In the playground, in the sharp autumn sunlight, the

only sound she could hear was the hydraulic wheezing of a digger on a nearby building site. Otherwise all was silent as the children stood to attention waiting for Myra to call them in, class by class.

6

Giving up her last full-time job was easy for Myra. Before the move to Little Pawnton all her waking hours had been split between work and Laura, with childminders guiltily organised, night-times spent with their daughter; by that time Myra did not have the energy for all the child demanded. She didn't know why she had gone on so long that way. Modern ethics, she used to think – being a working mother was almost the norm, it was *expected* of her. But part of the reason for their moving was that she might have Laura to herself during the day, every day. It was a prize to be snatched without reservation, something they should have done from the outset, both she and John agreed.

Then, John was senior architect in a strong young firm that had made the most of the boom years in the eighties. He had designed the big Darnley Insurance building in Stockport and won an award for it. He was respected for his work, achieving a success which rather amused him, and which he likened to being on a journey to some unknown destination he felt duty-bound to discover. If he disliked his new commuting duties, from village to city, he hid it well, cheerfully claiming he had got the time down to forty minutes each way, a figure checked each evening as part of a game with Laura who was almost four years old then, her baby blonde hair changing to a substantial brown.

Country life revealed a precocity in Laura that amazed Myra. It was a street wisdom she must have secretly gleaned in Manchester and at times it disarmed her mother, making her realise that whatever plans they might have for Laura, she was already capable of making up her own mind. It was a part of parenthood Myra had not suspected, had taken for granted in her teaching years, unaware of the subtle workings of a child's mind that would make her infinitely more sympathetic if she ever returned to her old job. John was probably the more natural parent, accepting Laura as she was, from the joyous day of her birth, tolerating her tantrums brilliantly, seducing the placid side of her with his endless patience. And to Myra, with her teaching experience an assumed qualification, fell the task of cautioning and cajoling. Her love affair with Laura was more of a secret, a sensuous thing fed by the impossibly soft skin of the child's hands and throat, the smell she made in the toilet – never repellent – and her hair, her clothes, the smallness of them, and the look in her eyes when she needed reassurance in a world that must have looked so big and threatening . . .

In order to get to know the Little Pawntonians, Myra made herself visible about the village, taking Laura daily to a weedy play area hidden almost apologetically behind the church. Here she talked with other mothers in the place, some, like Myra, displaced from the city. Their conversations were polite, wary, and centred almost exclusively on their respective children. Myra also made a point of habitual trips to the shop where she spent heavily despite there being a supermarket not fifteen minutes' drive away. Then there was the next-door neighbour, a thin dentured old stick called Ivy Malt who had a jolly and forgetful husband called Joe and a ratty black terrier. At first Laura was wary of the old woman, acting in a superior fashion in her company, talking about Daddy's important job, their two cars, the house they'd had in Manchester which was so, so big. This embarrassed Myra and she naturally offered the truth about their old life, rationalising Laura's comments, though Mrs Malt seemed smilingly impervious to any impudence on their daughter's part.

The old woman took a shine to them all, it seemed, waiting for Myra to hang washing in the garden so she could come out and hang her own things, the dog yapping at her heels. Her usual conversation began with a dig about the people from whom John and Myra had bought the house – a noisy young couple given to late-night entertaining and a sullenness in their dealings with local people. Myra would listen politely to the repeated tirades, careful not to take sides against the departed pair. Then once, when a sudden downpour came and Myra had to rush out, Mrs Malt, quite simultaneously, hurtled into her own garden, laughing heroically in the rain, still finding some means of berating her former neighbours while she snatched Joe's thermals from the line. Myra, back in the house, could not help laughing.

'What's the matter?' Laura asked.

'Nothing, dear. She's just so silly.'

'She is, isn't she? She's silly.' Laura aped her mother, laughing forcedly with her hand cupped over her mouth.

At the weekends there was usually something going on in the village, often organised by people like Myra and John with children to interest. There would be waste paper collections, nature trails, environmental meetings – minute events of heartbreaking insignificance when set against the affairs of the heedless revolving world beyond. And one bright summer week the church advertised a bring and buy sale for the coming Saturday. Did John want to go? Of course he did. It was expected of them, he said. A chance to tip a little coin into the villagers' coffers. Besides, it might be fun. The church bazaar. What could be more innocent?

What could? thought Myra . . .

The day they visited John's father was the day for putting the clocks back, a ritual Myra always detested. It snagged in her mind, this British event, this tampering with natural time, and she hated the thought of darkening afternoons, the endless winter nights. Perhaps that was the real reason she had thought of taking in a lodger – someone for company, to act as a foil against the turning of the seasons, the dying of the year.

The day itself was plain grey, the cloud cover unbroken from horizon to horizon as John drove them to the Wold Lodge residential home. This, a converted country house, was about ten miles to the east of York. It sat back from the main road, its lower half hidden by a gentle roll of the land. The upper floor, which could be seen from some way off, was covered in thick ivy that reached around the big bay windows to the house's elaborate brick cornices and mossy roof. It had once been a home for the rich and titled, the old money that had had to give way to the new. Now its residents were less than privileged, old hearts awaiting their final beat.

On the way there John chattered excitedly, sitting forward over the steering wheel, pulling out carelessly at one junction and causing a van to swerve, over-cautious at the next where an impatient queue formed behind him while he waited for the road to become absolutely clear.

When they reached the home he stood on the gravel drive patting his pockets, laughing nervously, saying he had forgotten to bring his money. It didn't matter, they both knew, the comment simply inspired by his anxiety, afloat now, as it always was on these occasions. Myra hooked her arm round his and led him inside.

The reception area was a long carpeted passage that smelt of furniture polish. A modern teak bureau had been built by the stairs to house a receptionist, though Myra had never seen anyone behind it. She slipped her arm out of John's, gave his wrist a reassuring squeeze, and pressed a button on the wall. This rang a bell somewhere beyond their hearing, the kind of bell that always left people with a doubt about having made their presence known. Within a minute though they were met by the nurse on duty, a plump, kindly-natured woman called Shirley who Myra thought may well have been older than many of the residents.

'Mr and Mrs Wentworth. Good to see you. Good to see you again.' She was out of breath, as if she had run to get there.

'Hello, er . . .' John began.

'Shirley. I see you've no head for names, Mr W. Not to worry. It's a problem for me too, these days. Something to do with the water, I always say. It's the chemicals they put in it. Not old age, mind.' She laughed nervously, thin lips parting to reveal lipstick smudges on her grey teeth.

'Quite,' said John, hanging back behind Myra's shoulder.

'And how has Bill been?' asked Myra, who always did the asking.

'Oh, the same, really. He gets along, you know. Not the noisiest of fellows, of course, but he seems comfortable. Sleeps a lot. But eats well. Very fond of the ice cream,' she said, again with the icy humour, adjusting the cruelly tight belt of her uniform as if to let the laughter out a little more easily. 'Shall I show you up, then?'

'Yes,' said Myra. 'Thank you.'

They followed her up the long straight staircase, pausing

with her while she checked the precarious-looking chairlift at the top of the stairs. Then a door opened in the hall below and a small old woman emerged, wiping her hands on her apron. Shirley tutted.

'And what'll it be now, Mrs Coyle?' she said, leaning over the banister.

The woman jumped, startled by the voice over her head.

'I was just wondering if I should set the tables, Shirley,' she said, still looking in front of her, unable to locate the nurse's voice. 'Is it time?'

'Away with you, Peggy. Lunch isn't for another two hours yet. What's the point in doing the tables now? The cutlery'll only go walkabout.'

'Just wondering, that's all,' said the woman, looking vacantly towards the big front door.

'Well, don't wonder,' Shirley said firmly. 'Go back in the lounge. I'll be down in a minute.'

'If you say so.'

'I do say so, Peggy. I do.'

The woman humphed and went back into the room.

'Another fifteen minutes and she'll be asking the same thing,' said Shirley. 'Then it'll be every five minutes, then every five seconds. Still, keeps her occupied, yes?'

Myra smiled sympathetically.

They followed the nurse along the landing where one of the doors was open revealing an empty room with a stripped bed, an open wardrobe, the window wide to a misty scroll of ploughed fields and the distant wolds. Myra wondered if someone had died. John stopped to look through the door. She wished he hadn't. He caught up with her as Shirley knocked pointedly at the door to Bill's room. They all waited a second before the nurse nodded and led them in.

Bill was in his usual place in an armchair by the bed.

He was wearing a red pullover and a thick woollen dressing-gown over his pyjamas. One foot was slippered and resting on the floor, the other bare and stretched out in front of him. Shirley bent down effortfully to put the stray slipper back on, pressing his leg to get the foot to stay on the floor. He had been shaved that morning, though the electric razors they used always left a silvery film, a magnet for food scraps and bits of dried skin. There was a small table in front of him, its tubular frame caught beneath the leg of the chair so he could not tip it over. On a chest of drawers was a cereal bowl caked with its half-remaining contents, and next to this was a portable television showing a children's pop magazine programme. Shirley went over to the television and turned the volume down. Then she went back to Bill. She ran her hand through his thick white hair.

'And how's William today?' she said loudly. 'Look who's here. Look who's come to see you. Your son and his lovely wife. Aren't you pleased to see them?'

The old man made a chewing motion, putting his fat tongue out. He raised his foot in front of him again.

Myra looked at John, his closed eyes, the strawberry mark glowing on his cheek. This was how it took him, every time – the unavoidable loss of composure, the looseness of the jowls, the sadness, the guilt. Shirley saw his expression and smiled wanly.

'I'll leave you alone then,' she said to Myra. 'Goodness knows what they'll be getting up to downstairs.'

'Thank you,' said Myra.

When the nurse had gone Myra looked round for the footstool she usually used and pulled it up to sit beside Bill. John went and stood by the window while Myra chatted one-sidedly with the old man, feeding him the fondant mints she remembered him liking, before the silence that had come to claim him as one of its own.

*　　*　　*

In the car on the way back Myra's sympathy for John thinned, giving way to impatience.

'You could have made the effort. You can't even bring yourself to speak to him.'

'I can't talk to him. How can I?'

'He's your father.'

'That's not him. That's not the father I remember.'

'Still – '

'Still nothing,' he snapped. 'He's not there. He's not in there. We could be bloody spacemen for all he knows. What's the point in going? What's the point in any of it?'

Myra felt a familiar weariness, a well-known line of conversation waiting to be taken up, the words barely changing each time they followed it. Her own father had died when she was sixteen . . .

Her father. Who had fought in the war, who had survived two years in a concentration camp, who had stayed in the Army and made it to Captain, who painted watercolour butterflies. Who, a week before he was due to retire, took a routine exercise on a firing range where a rookie claimed to have received a revelation from St Paul and threw down his gun, making it fire, the bullet, in all the spaces of the world it could fly through, finding its way to her father's heart, two hundred yards away. Bull's-eye. A farce, a tragedy . . .

And she had let the grief pour out of her, had worn it with pride, at school, at home, until it no longer existed. That's what you did, that's how you handled it – you bled a little, a lot if need be. Then you let the wound heal. Hadn't John been through it before, with his mother? The affectionate way he still talked about her revealed no guilt, none of the complexities that bothered him now. But maybe this was different. How do you grieve for someone who is still alive?

'Your trouble is you blame yourself,' said Myra. 'Why should you?'

'It happened at the same time as everything else. It all came at once. We drove him over the edge, do you know that?'

'Rubbish. It was a coincidence, that's all.'

'Too much of a coincidence. Too bloody much.' He cuffed the steering wheel, then breathed deeply, trying to restrain himself. 'It's . . . I don't know. Someone paying us back. That's what it is. Some twisted . . . evil . . .'

'You're being ridiculous again. It's a purely physical thing. An act of God . . .'

'So that's who's behind it.'

'It's an illness,' said Myra, resisting her temper. 'Why don't you look it up in a book? Maybe then you won't feel so bad.'

'Maybe I need to feel bad. Maybe it's the only way I know how to cope. It's my curse. Bad me. Maybe I deserve it.'

Myra looked ahead at the flat dull land, the farm silos, the electricity pylons, then the bypass and the first houses of the arriving town, the suburban superstores, the Minster sitting lordly above it all, a piece of ancient England, airborne, its towers grey-pink in the hard white light. She was tiring, wishing she could get out of the car, John's car, where he was usually alone thinking these private bitter thoughts. For a moment Myra believed she did not know him at all.

'That's stupid,' she said.

7 ∫

The church fête at Little Pawnton was a bigger event than they had imagined. Families came from outlying farms and other villages, all drawn by the hot bright day. And local people appeared whom they had not seen before, suggesting a secret dimension, an enclave of the village to which outsiders were not invited.

It was held in the church grounds where there was a long black hut, used mostly for parish council meetings. The inside of the hut was painted a grubby mint colour and it had a sagging chipboard ceiling with a Union Jack at one end that the Scouts saluted on their night during the week. Myra, in her summer whites and sandals, wandered the stalls while John, sweating idiotically in his wax coat and boots, took Laura to look round the rows of tables and a red and white striped marquee on the lawns outside. The wares on offer varied from suspiciously neat 'hand-carved' figurines to hopeful heaps of clothing and worn-out shoes. Myra paused at a collection of old glass ornaments, trying to visualise any item that might fit in their living-room, passing on to a box of books whose every title she examined without interest. Then John was back, standing behind her grinning, blowing a drop of sweat from the tip of his nose. In his arms was a heavy wooden box with black metal corners and a big old key in its lock.

'Look at this!' he said. 'Belonged to the church. The real thing. You'll have to come and look. There's tons of good stuff out there.'

'All right.' She looked over his shoulder, searching among the legs of the old ladies and farmers who were filling the place. 'Where's Laura?'

'Look.' He opened the lid of the box with a struggle. 'There's a secret compartment. There, in the bottom.'

'John, where is Laura?'

'Isn't she here?'

'No. Of course she's not here.'

'She said she'd come back on her own to find you.'

Myra flushed with irritation.

'Well, she hasn't found me, has she? She's too young to be wandering around on her own. John . . .'

'All right, all right.' He put the box down, still with a maddening regard for its finer points. 'She'll be here somewhere.'

Myra bit her tongue, her anger rising against this whole silly place, this idyll, the twee notion that had brought them to the country. Then she began to panic.

'We've got to find her. Laura? Laura?'

Her calls drew a watching attention from a few individuals milling about the room, standing behind stalls, their personalities suddenly changed to Myra. Now they were not silly, but concerned, intelligent people whose integrity would be unimpeachable, whom Myra could turn to for help. She bumped into a woman turning a china vase in her hand, the door to the outside seeming a day's journey away.

'Careful,' John said, somewhere behind her, still locked in his unforgivable indifference.

On the lawn outside peace still reigned, horribly. Myra searched among the children playing hide and seek beneath the trestle-tables, calling her daughter's name, her face wet with tears. The fine summer day became transformed into something grotesque, fair weather that she might never be able to face again. In a single isolated moment Myra believed this, seeing herself as a grieving hag, hiding from the sunlight, a witch to frighten the children at play, as she was doing now in her furious stooped tour of the grass, the tables, her searching in the marquee among the lower halves of adult bodies, behind boxes, anything of a size that might conceal her child . . .

'At eight in the morning the two Sheriffs came for her. And she was ready for them. She had already sent her hat to her husband as a token of her loving duty to him. And to her eldest daughter Anne she sent her hose and shoes as symbols of her wish that she follow in her virtuous steps in the service of God.

'Margaret wanted Yoward's wife to see her die. And it was her express wish that some good Catholics might be with her in the last agony of her betrothal to the Lord, to put her in remembrance of Him. Yoward's wife said that she would not see her die so cruel a death for all York, but she would arrange for good friends to lay weights on her that she might be quickly delivered from pain.

'The walk from the prison to the Tollbooth (the office of the collector of bridge tolls and an occasional meeting place for the Corporation) was said to be only six or seven yards. But the way was difficult, huge crowds having gathered in the streets. Fawcett, the Sheriff in charge of the execution, tried to hasten the barefooted Margaret's passage through the hordes, but she would not be hurried, turning to him with the words: ''Good Master Sheriff, let me deal my poor alms before I now go, for my time is but short.''

'And all who saw her were said to have marvelled at the joyful radiance in her face.'

Myra sat back from the book and massaged her neck. It was the third version of the story she had found. Originally she had set herself the task of reading the entire history of

York as a way of ingratiating herself with the city, albeit only academically. But she had soon become bogged down with the dryness of historical detail, troop movements, the politics, the dates and facts that simply sat there. Then she had found the story of Margaret Clitherow, poor Margaret, and it had held her, moved her, Myra, an agnostic. The notion of faith had rarely concerned her throughout her life and she saw no possibility of a dramatic conversion now. Yet there was something in this story, something meant for her, a vast philosophy that Myra – late twentieth century, peaceable, safe – felt the need to address. But now it was late and she was tired. She closed the book, unwilling to go on, unable to consider fully the cruelty in its conclusion.

The rest of the library was empty save for a shuffling young man reading a train-spotter's monthly and a girl in bondage gear writing feverishly in the law section. These and the man by the desk were the only other occupants of the big room, a scarcity of people that seemed to invite an abuse of the silence rule with the use of normal voices instead of whispers.

Myra closed her eyes. It was the day after they had visited John's father and she had been determined not to let it be wasted. John, still in a mood, had gone off on a drive and maybe it was better to just leave him that way for now. He would come round again, given a few days. Alex was his usual sunny-humoured self and seemed to have forgotten his quaint little come-on with Myra earlier in the week. On that front the previous harmony had been easily restored, but today he was out and the evening, if John was late back, stretched dreary and empty before Myra. Perhaps she might take a book home with her, force her mind to try once more to absorb the history of the town. Then a vaguely remembered saying floated into her tired head, something about how the only way you could truly know a place was by seeing its effect on the lives of the people who lived there.

Place and effect. The moors in high summer, distant unforgotten limestone crags, brilliant skies criss-crossed with vapour trails, the endless space that kept its secrets, that yielded to no human endeavour, that mocked her keening . . .

Myra opened her eyes.

And remembered.

She was standing in the middle of the lawn, at her full height, her expression quite wretched. People were passing by, oblivious to her, to the sudden history of their loss. She felt faint. Where was John? How could he take this so calmly? The fool, the fool. Then she saw him as if through a tunnel that had been carved in the hot air between them. He was laughing, and Myra could hear this laughter to the brief exclusion of all other sound. The murmurs of the people around her returned as she recognised Mrs Malt with Joe and the dog, and Laura waving a lecturing finger the dog was trying to bite.

'OK?' said John when Myra reached them. He was trying to hide his heavy breathing, smiling but with wide fierce eyes that told Myra he had begun to worry as much as her.

'Yes.' She dried the wetness from her cheeks as discreetly as possible. 'Where have you been, you scamp?'

'We had to take Ben outside; didn't we?' said Mrs Malt.

'Yes,' said Laura. 'He did a big pooh on the grass. It was like a sausage. You're a very naughty dog, aren't you, Benjy?'

'Well, crisis over then,' John said, aside to Myra. 'Would you like to, er, you know, the stall I mentioned?'

'Yes,' said Myra, glad of the chance to move away.

'Come along, Laura,' said John with mock severity. 'Take Daddy's hand.'

When they were out of the Malts' hearing John let out a long-held sigh.

'Are you all right?' he asked.

'Yes. You?'

'I am now. Had me a bit worried, though. For a moment.'

'I know. Me too. Shall we go?'

'I don't know. Well . . .' He looked down at Laura who had seen a corner with games for children, a part of the area Myra had recently searched, her mind then perfectly oblivious to its function. 'Maybe we could hang around a bit. Another ten minutes or so.'

'All right.'

Two hours later, with the sun high and burning, they were still there. A dance band arrived and played on the lawn, and meals and drinks were being served in the marquee. Tables were cleared for people to sit at and before they really thought about it Myra and John had been there the whole afternoon, following the unknown agenda, John getting a little drunk on beer. This translated itself into his buying a stack of things: four old stools he intended to renovate, the wooden box, a table missing its glass top, a heavy mirror that was once part of a dressing-table. He deposited the lot in a heap in one corner of the lawn, standing by it now and again with a merry grin. The vicar came up to him carrying a big old walkie-talkie with which he was presumably running the event. John made what Myra thought was a stupid joke about the man having rung up God on the thing for the good weather. But the vicar, a lean, preserved man of indistinguishable age, laughed surprisingly loudly. He then politely offered the history of the stools and the box which had actually been given by a parishioner for the vicarage, but for which they had never found any practical use. John listened with exaggerated interest, before a crackling message on the walkie-talkie took the clergyman away.

At first Myra had thought John was being eccentric and it might cause tongues to wag, but she simply helped herself to one or two drinks and let the day take her mood, the incident with Laura forgotten, dismissed as the kind of thing that happened at least once in the life of every child.

As the sun fell, colouring the hills a glorious gold, people began making their way home leaving a hard core of redoubtable women church supporters clearing the last of the tables, and a few drinkers collecting in knots by the hut and the entrance to the marquee. The band struck up again, playing loosely, some of its members a bit the worse for wear. Myra and John sat at the table nearest John's purchases, Laura in her mother's arms, vainly trying to fend off her tiredness. John was staring intently at a half-empty glass as if he were about to ask it a deep question.

'Well, perhaps we should go,' said Myra.

'Mmm. Maybe.'

'How are you going to get that lot home?' she said, nodding at the pile.

'No idea.' He laughed with a splutter that betrayed his drunkenness.

By the open door of the hut was a group of four men. One of them, Myra noticed, had been watching John for a while and now he was coming forward, smiling.

'Got your bike with you?' He pointed at John's things.

'No, I haven't,' said John, grinning. 'Don't know what we're going to do. Open to suggestions, really.'

'Well, don't you worry about that lot.'

'Oh?'

'I can get my lad round with the pick-up. He'll drop it off for you.'

'That's very decent of you,' said John, revived by the possibility of extending his patronage to the community.

'It's nothing. We help each other round here. Have to. You're at South Cottage, aren't you? The one at the end, next to old Joe and Ivy?'

'Yes,' said Myra. 'We're newcomers, I'm afraid.'

'That's all right by me. No need to bother about that. I've seen you around anyway, you know, your house. And I'd been wondering . . . Mind if I join you?'

'No, no,' said John. 'Please do. You were wondering about what?'

'Your garden. That tree that blew down just after you moved in.'

Myra's heart sank a little with the thought that they had been watched so closely. She had always tried to maintain an air of respectful anonymity, attracting the attention of no one she chose not to deal with.

'You're not a gardener too, are you?' John asked.

'I'm not, no. Though my lad is.'

He was fiftyish, thickset and weatherbeaten. He was wearing a grubby cream jumper, jeans, and a navy beanie hat from under which his hair strayed in tangled curls. His name was Chuck and he began telling them about himself. His first comment was about his working on the farm at the top approach to the village. His next comment was about his brother-in-law who had worked there too and who died there last year when a grit hopper he was working under fell on him. It was a powerful remark, out of the blue, intended to hold some significance for them, thought Myra. Or perhaps this was just the way they revealed themselves, unmethodically, disarmingly, country people who knew what time you went to bed.

His family was typical of the area, hardly any work for the kids save for the farms or the lucky few who got jobs with local services. He had four children, the oldest three all having married and moved away, to Liverpool in one case, Huddersfield and Leeds the other two. It grieved him, really. His was one of the village's oldest families, but that counted for nothing now. He knew barely half the people in the place these days, new blood like Myra and John never seeming to want to stay for long. Then he steadied his criticism, tempering it with a statement of tolerance – 'But you're all right. You'll do for me.' Myra could not quite believe in this. Perhaps he was only realising their usefulness to him, smelling their money.

The youngest son was called Danny, nineteen, a willing lad but a bit backward. Chuck had managed to get him work now and then on the farm, but it was never for long – his boss just couldn't afford him. Still, he was a good lad, Danny. Didn't deserve the dole. And he was good with the soil, uncannily so. He just knew how things grew. John, anxious to take this bait, pre-empted him.

'So, he can help us out, can he?'

'Can do,' Chuck said, a little warily, as if this had all been too easy.

'And if we paid cash – no receipts, no pack drill – that would be all right, would it?' said John.

Chuck smiled, vulgarly satisfied, believing perhaps that he really had put one over on the newcomers.

'That would be about right. Leave your stuff here and I'll send him round with it, Monday. You can see him then.'

'All right,' said John.

Chuck went back to talk with his friends who had been watching them all along and who took it in turns to look round again at Myra and John.

'Seems reasonable,' said John. 'What do you think?'

'Well, I don't know,' said Myra, feeling a very real sense of reserve. And swallowing it, for his sake. 'We could use the help I suppose. Yes, why not?'

'Why not,' John repeated, pleased with himself, taking a few last mouthfuls of his flat beer.

They walked home in the fragrant air of twilight, John carrying the sleeping Laura. And when they had put her to bed, shushing away the last of her tired protests, they went to their own room congratulating each other on a perfect day, on their wisdom in moving there, on their penetration, as John saw it, of the secret heart of the village. Then they undressed each other and lay down giggling, making love slowly, half in sleep, the silent blue hills standing in witness through the open window . . .

8

Over the next two weeks John's mood swung back to the taut cheerfulness of recent times. He did not mention Bill at all. When Myra thought back to the relationship John used to have with his father she remembered no complications, no grain of antagonism or resentment. Perhaps there had been some unspeakable act, a tangle of darkness that could never be unravelled? It seemed unlikely. Bill had always been the gentle and easy type, though Myra suspected a concealed, greater intelligence that, in his job at the railway offices, he had never been able to use fully. In John the powers of intellect flourished – he had been much more successful than his father. Maybe that was it, the burden, the guilt of achievement.

Myra settled readily into the routine at Bowhandy, looking forward to each morning's work, easily eluding the little grouses and knockbacks that all teachers had at some time. Kate seemed the hardbitten sort, mercurial, but Rowena and Andrew were reliable. And Myra was working well, more and more of her old abilities returning each day, the pratfalls, the manipulative ploys of the children something she could read before they happened. She was a better teacher than before, her new-found maturity a source of sparkling satisfaction to her. And when the weekend came, and with it the half-term holiday, she felt frustration and a nagging fear of slipping back into the darkness, the desperation of the earlier part of the year.

On Saturday evening, with Alex away again, Myra and John went to a recital of Monteverdi madrigals at a brand new community hall across town. The tickets were complimentary – John's firm had designed the place – and as they dressed and made ready to go, he seemed pleasingly enthusiastic about the evening, suggesting a few drinks and a meal to follow. It was the sort of thing they went to years ago, only occasionally, but often enough for 'the cull-cher', as John disparagingly called it, to work as an antidote to the ceaseless noise of modern times. But when they got there they found themselves over-dressed, the audience numbering less than twenty, and the acoustics deadening, drawing unhappy asides from the singers, a local amateur group. Half-way through the fourth piece they stalled completely, one woman moaning openly about the lack of atmosphere, and the event began fraying into an embarrassing calamity. John swallowed his unease. Myra could have dismissed the evening as merely regrettable, but afterwards John insisted on going straight home. There he put on a Sting cassette, humming the tunes loudly as he poured himself a large scotch. 'We'll not bother again,' he said, smiling but not hiding his disappointment over the night. Then he went quiet, turning off the tape in favour of the television which he stared at wall-eyed until the early hours.

On Monday, with Alex still away, John went to work as usual leaving Myra alone in the house. It was raining constantly. She wrote a long letter to her mother, dealing in her usual polite tone with the external details of her life, her job, John's work, the state of his father's health for which a platitude of the nursing home sufficed – he was as comfortable as he could be. She did not mention Alex, thinking he might not last long with them anyway, and knowing how tiresome it would be having to explain to her mother the reasons for taking in a guest at all. With the morning barely half over she set about doing all the washing she could find, then scraped the grime from the cooker and Hoovered the stairs. At one o'clock she felt the television calling her to her old place in the living-room. She watched the first fifteen minutes of an American business-power soap in which one of the characters had her pomposity underscored with a grotesque parody of the English accent. Myra turned it off. She didn't need this any more. She had life now, real and regained. With the rain having stopped, at least for a while, she put on her coat with the idea of posting the letter and wandering up into town.

At Bootham Bar a guide was pointing out the portcullis to a crowd of Italian tourists. He paused, looking satisfied as a ripple of laughter spread among his audience. Myra stepped into the road and past them, carrying on to the Minster and its windy forecourt where the pavement artists had abandoned their rain-smudged efforts in favour of the pub. From there she went along Low Petergate and into King's Square where a nickelodeon was playing and a hot-potato wagon was enjoying its busiest spell of the day. Her target was The Shambles where she had half a mind to visit the shrine of Margaret Clitherow, but at the door she stopped, restrained by the idea of simply 'popping in' to such a holy place. She hovered in the narrow street, the low shop windows drawing her attention, the smell of their goods – woollens, leather, chocolate – mingling faintly on the moist air, seducing in her the urge to spend. She loved shopping, of course, though her buying habits had always been predetermined and she did not like the thought of its becoming the obsession that it could be these days. Recently she had read that sixty per cent of twenty to twenty-five-year-olds preferred shopping to sex. This had staggered her. Was she missing out on something? When had she started being old-fashioned?

At the end of The Shambles Myra turned along Pavement and up into the wider spaces of Parliament Street with its funny new loos and fountains, its crowds of people, children loose in the half-term holiday, students looking for somewhere to chain their bikes. Then, in a department store window, she saw a black calf-length skirt teamed with a tangerine corduroy waistcoat, pink satin blouse, cowboy boots. And suddenly the shopping thing clicked in her mind. Want and acquisition. The cultivation of those qualities, the way they afforded immunity from moral predicaments, affirmed one's existence, buying the world to be of the world. I shop, therefore I am. John knew all about this and he hated it. But it was in Myra to be that way, to make herself open to an education in materialism, the cult of it now seeping into her skin from the soft Yorkshire air. She could want that outfit, could want it now, to buy it now with the money she had made herself from her work, her efforts. Her work, her wants. Her reward, this. The need became real, feverish. Tomorrow would not do. She could not come back tomorrow and feel this same desire. That would have been the old Myra's careful way. This was a moment to be completely herself. More so, someone new. She stepped up to the store window. She wanted that look. It was meant for her. It had been put there to *save* her. It was too young, of course, and ridiculously expensive. But Myra wanted to pay the price, to suffer John's sardonic looks when he saw it, to commit every folly going. Then, as she reached in her bag to check for her purse, the feeling died a little. Even as she stood back for a better look, credit card in hand, seeing the ensemble as yet more handsome and perfect for her, the desire was poised before the flames.

How could she submit to this kind of spontaneity? Where would it all end?

'So what's with the long faces?' said Alex.

'No long faces here,' said John, feeling the shape of his head. 'No. Fairly round this. Conforms rather well with the universal design. Not long, not by any stretch of the imagination. Myra's perhaps is a little . . . what, protracted? A bit on the long side? This evening, anyway. Touch of the glums, dear?'

Myra shrugged. 'No. Winter coming. Maybe that's it.'

Alex straightened himself on his chair.

'Ask me what sort of a day I've had,' he said. 'Go on. Ask.'

'All right,' said John. 'Well, Alex, how was it? What have you achieved on this God-given day, this fraction, albeit dreary, of Man's time on this planet? Tell, tell.'

'Call me smart,' said Alex, head set smugly. 'Call me a cool operator.'

'A job?' said Myra.

'That's it. Got it in one.'

'But that's wonderful news. Congratulations.'

'Yes, well done,' said John, the wind taken out of his cynical sails.

'Come on then, tell us about it,' said Myra.

'Parkside Investment and Insurance. You must have heard of it.'

'Can't say I have.' John pinched his lip as if to keep his sense of mischief at bay. 'Where's the office?'

'Ah, they've got places everywhere. And I mean everywhere. National. No local outfit. They've just opened this place off Skeldergate. That's where I'll be based.'

'And what exactly will you be doing?' asked Myra.

'Life insurance, pension schemes, that sort of stuff. Start next Monday.'

'You'd be giving . . . advice?' said John, with a lift of the eyebrows that Myra did not like.

'Sort of. Yeah. Chasing up leads. Bit of cold selling to start with, they said, help them get established in the area. But that's all right. It's a job, isn't it?' Alex said defensively. 'I'll just have to be sharper than the next man. Put my back into it. I can do that. Know it.' He was pointing his finger at John as if he were still in the interview, trying to sell himself. And it was then that Myra realised he was wearing a tie, a crumpled narrow paisley thing with the thin end pulled longer than the broad. He was wearing it with the green shirt he had worn the night he arrived.

'Good. Well, great,' said John.

'Yeah. It'll be good.'

Then, as if insecure about their response to his news, Alex began shoring it up with talk about basic salary grades: nothing much to speak of, not to start with, but after a year or so . . . And until then, well, the commissions they were offering – fantastic. He elaborated on each point, starting in contrived reflection, emptying his head of what seemed to be his entire and limited knowledge of the work, eventually working his way round to the amount of money he expected to make.

'Well,' said John. 'This time next year and it'll be managing director, eh?'

Alex laughed, enjoying the comment.

'Could be. Or area manager. That's the next step.'

Myra smiled warmly.

'Whatever happens,' she said, 'I'm sure you'll enjoy it.'

'Mmm.' He sat back, pursing his lips demurely, the docker's-grab hands flat on the table. 'There's just one small problem.'

'And what's that?' said John, yawning.

'This week. Cash-flow wise. The rent, I mean.'

'Oh?'

'I'm a bit light. Till I get paid.'

'Till you get paid,' John said, scepticism renewed. 'And that would be when? Next week?'

'That could be it.'

'I see.'

It was a moment Myra had often imagined, yet hoped would never come. They had become so used to Alex's company that the business side of the arrangement had become subverted. It was in her to say that the money didn't matter, that he could skip a week if he liked. But there was John, picking at his teeth, looking older, the man of the house, heading for one of his coloured moods.

'No money then,' John said, glancing at the side of his plate as if looking for misplaced coins.

'No. But I'll see you straight. Honest. Not like me to owe people.'

'Well . . .' said John, frowning, making a small agony of the moment.

If he let Myra down now she would not forgive him. What did the money matter? When did it ever matter if things were going well?

'Maybe . . .' said John, stroking his nose, '. . . for this one week, we could think of a few things that need doing round the house. Maybe you could earn your keep that way, for now anyway. What do you think, Myra?'

'I think that's a very good idea. The back yard needs straightening. And the attic,' she said, looking for more ways to reinforce the suggestion before John changed his mind.

'Sounds great,' said Alex.

'Right,' said John, standing. 'I'll leave it up to you, Myra.' He remained where he was, quiet for a few seconds as if pondering the wisdom of his idea. Then he smiled effetely. 'I'll be going up now. Old age, Alex. It gets to you in the end. It'll get to you too, one day.'

Alex sniggered, not knowing what to make of the remark. 'Goodnight, John.'

'Yes. Goodnight, Alex.'

When he had gone, Alex turned to Myra and she saw the relief, and a little impudence, in his eyes.

'Why did he say that? About being old? He's not that old. Can't be.'

'I don't know,' said Myra. 'I've not heard him say it before. He's probably just tired. Anyway, how does his suggestion suit you? There is plenty needs doing about the place. Do you mind?'

'Nah. Suits me fine. I'll start now, with this lot,' he said, nodding at the dishes on the table.

Myra laughed.

'That wasn't quite what I had in mind. Still, you can dry while I wash, if you like.'

'Sure. Let's do it.'

Myra laughed again as he stood and began swiping pots to the sink.

'What's so funny?' he asked.

'Nothing. Just you. You make me laugh, sometimes.'

'Does you good to laugh. You're more attractive when you smile. Did you know that?'

The remark surprised Myra. It was honestly meant, but it carried a misguided weight, a frivolity she did not have the energy to deal with.

'Everyone looks better when they're happy,' she said. 'You'll find the tea-towel over there. On the hook.'

*   *   *

'Thank you. For being tactful.'

The street outside was quiet save for the odd car rattling a loose manhole cover as it swished along the top road. Myra rested her hand on John's warm bare shoulder. He flinched.

'Did you hear something?' he said.

'No.'

'A scratching noise. In the attic. You must have heard it.'

'Sorry.' Myra kissed his skin. 'Didn't hear a thing.'

John took a deep, weary breath.

'Should have caught the thing by now. Maybe if I moved the trap up there, or bought another one.'

Myra smiled, resting her head against his arm. She had quite forgotten about the mouse, his mouse. She made a mental note to look for signs of its residence in the food cupboards. If she caught it, or at least managed to see it, it might mean something to him. She stroked the inside of his arm and licked his ear lobe. It was an old signal, an overture to intimacy practised since the early days, developed to a point by which they could bypass the encumbrance of words.

'Were you all right down there, you and Alex?' he asked.

'Fine. I think he was rather relieved that we weren't just going to throw him out.' But she did not want to talk. She took his hand and pressed it on her stomach, easing herself close so that the length of her body lay over half of his. She pushed her toes under his, kissing and running her hands over the downy skin of his chest, beneath his arms.

But he did not respond. Myra could see his empty expression in the half-light. She hugged him again and curled his pubic hair round her fingers.

'It's been ages,' she said.

'I know. I'm sorry. I just don't feel, I don't know, the

need these days. And it's not fair, not fair on you. Another of my failings.'

'You're too hard on yourself. Just relax.'

She slipped her arm round his shoulders and drew him gently to her.

'Have you seen Alex?' John said. 'The funny way he looks at you?'

'I hadn't noticed.'

He chuckled. 'Sort of hangdog.'

'Really?' But she wasn't listening. She rubbed her cheek in his neck, working on him again, sure that with a little effort they could just skip over this problem.

'Listen, I wouldn't mind, you know . . .'

'What wouldn't you mind?' She was kneading his stomach with the palm of her hand.

'If you wanted someone else. In bed.'

'What?' Myra pulled sharply away. 'I don't believe I heard that. What do you think I am? How can you suggest such a thing?'

'You have needs. It occurred to me, that's all.'

'It occurred to you.'

'Yes.'

Myra groaned, her wish for intimacy turning to poison in her stomach, being used against her, perversely. She lay on her back, closed her eyes and opened them again.

'When are you going to stop all this? When are you going to stop driving us apart? There's no need. You mustn't carry on like this.'

The following minutes were loaded with a need for talk, for hours of explanation. But Myra knew that when he was in this kind of mood the argument might lead to a catastrophic end. Her mind was turning like a boiling sea, her usual sense of logic so stirred and unruly that it was impossible to find the right thing to say. All she could manage was: 'Please don't say things like that. You don't mean it. You don't know what I want.'

And she lay on her side with her back to him, stifling in the silence.

9

Myra remembered Danny's arrival well. On the day after the fête they walked the moors in the enduring sunshine, John jokingly remarking that they might never see the things he had bought again. But on Monday morning the boy was there.

John had gone to work and Myra remembered being startled by the knock at the back door. Since there was no gate, whoever it was must have climbed over the garden wall. Her heart was beating sharply as she opened the door to find this youth standing there. He had small eyes and puffy cheeks – the result of Pawntonian genetics? But he was thin, the nippy sort, and shorter than Myra had imagined that big man's son might be.

'Danny?'

He hesitated before nodding, as if unsure of his own name.

'I brought your stuff. From Saturday.'

'Yes. Of course.'

'Can I use the front?'

'I don't see much point in your dragging it over the wall, do you?' She was calmer now, annoyed that he should have surprised her this way.

She showed him through the house and waited while he brought the things from the van. Laura sat on the stairs watching him stack the bits and pieces in the hallway.

'There's the garden,' he said when he had finished. 'You want some work doing.'

There was a reluctance in the tone of his voice. Myra imagined the gruff figure of his father lingering somewhere in his recent memory, telling him to get to work. She took him back through the house.

'Well, there it is,' she said, more cheerfully, Laura standing behind her on the doorstep, peering round her knees. 'There's the bit at the front as well, but it's this we're most concerned about.' She pointed to the tree. 'It needs shifting. Can you do that?'

Danny looked down at the tree lying among the rye grass and thistles, its branches like the outstretched arms of someone asking to be saved from the choking undergrowth. He sucked through his small teeth.

'I'll need a branch cutter. You got one?'

'No. Sorry.'

'I'll have to fetch ours, then.'

And with that he went, climbing back over the wall with one easy pull at the top.

'What's he going to do?' asked Laura.

'He's going to clear the garden.'

'Couldn't you do that?'

'We probably could, come to think of it,' Myra said, doubtful about the boy.

After two hours he had still not returned. Myra's reservations deepened and she wondered if she could find some way of saying that the tree was the only real job they had for him. It was gone twelve o'clock when he came back, not bothering to announce himself. Myra heard the rasp of the saw and went out to find he had already severed the main branches, cutting the larger pieces into logs of a uniform length which he stacked in a neat pile by the wall. As he worked he chattered to himself occasionally, looking both absorbed and irritated by his task. He did not stop, even when a fine short drizzle began, nor did he acknowledge Mrs Malt's presence in the next garden, the old woman coming right up to the adjoining wall then turning away, her expression a little pale and concerned.

Laura took no notice of the activity until she became bored with the game she was playing and climbed on an armchair to watch Danny through the window.

'He's silly,' she said, 'working in the rain.'

'Yes.'

'He'll get all wet. He'll catch a cold.'

'He might,' said Myra, ironing for want of something better to make her look occupied when the boy had finished.

'Can I go out and watch him, when it's stopped raining?'

'He might not want you in the way, darling.'

Laura sighed.

'What will he do with all the branches? Will he take them for his fire?'

'I've no idea.'

'Will he have a fire at his house? A real one?'

'I really don't know,' Myra said tetchily, wondering what was nibbling at her nerves that morning.

She ushered Laura away from the window and into the dining-room for lunch. Ten minutes later she heard a crackling noise and smelt smoke filtering into the house. Laura, with no curiosity for this, carried on playing with her meal while Myra went back into the lounge to see a ball of flame rising from the heap of twigs Danny had made in the centre of the garden. He was standing by, watching, shepherding the outer unburnt material to the centre of the flames with a stick. Myra went out to him.

'Will you burn it all?'

'Just this stuff. Nothing else for it.'

'What about the rest?'

But he said nothing, wiping the grime on his forehead, the dull eyes livened by a flurry of flame to one side of the fire's structure. Mrs Malt made an appearance at her kitchen window, closing it noisily and backing away . . .

By Friday of the half-term week Myra's spirits began to lift. In the afternoon she went to town to pay bills and draw money from the bank. And she went to the store again where the outfit she had seen was still in the window. She could buy it now and use the new look against John. But why? Why play his silly game and make things worse? What was he after anyway? Separation? A divorce? This would be his first extreme suggestion, if he made any comment at all about what was really on his mind. Over the last few days he had remained quiet, living with his carefully concealed thoughts. Myra, tiring of his silences, went through hour-long phases of considering their splitting up as an option, a plain possibility, calculating how she might make a life for herself, where she might go, the money she would need. Then, when the day stretched a little longer, she was dismayed by these thoughts, wanting John home so she could apologise for the ideas in her head. He would have to be the one to suggest such a thing. And it seemed he would never be able to – on current form, neither of them would. She looked at the dummy, at its eternal coy glance, at the clothes which looked seedy now. This was one of her rational hours. Old Myra was back, sensible and patient, and maybe she wasn't so bad after all. She looked scornfully at the dummy then walked away, smiling.

It was only three thirty but lights were on in high office windows, the traffic was beginning its first exodus from city car-parks, and the air was tangy with cold. Myra made her way back by the river where the only boat was an old barge tethered near the Museum Gardens, its bleached green canopy strewn with wet leaves. When she reached the turning that led up to their street she carried on walking, feeling the need to stay a while longer in the daylight, that refined light of late October which might reflect her mellow mood quite reasonably.

Passing under Clifton Bridge she came to the Ings where the sun was falling and the shadows of the trees reached infinitely across the golden pastures. Here people were walking dogs and kids were testing the fortitude of their mountain bikes by bouncing them up and down the flood bank. After half a mile or so, when she was past the sugar factory on the far bank, Myra felt an agreeable tiredness that meant she would sleep well tonight. She found an old log to sit on and looked down at a line of dried foam and twiggy debris that marked the extent of a recent flood. Beyond this, bars of silver birch trunks were standing in sharp resolution against the river which moved gently behind them, its ripples black and bronze in the dying light. It was tranquillity itself, the perfect scene, an eternal moment such as the heart craved, but the mind could never fully accept. Myra wondered about this until, shivering with the cold, she pushed the thought away in favour of the more practical consideration about what she should prepare for dinner.

A few solitary walkers passed by in their private moods and Myra decided to wait until the last of them had gone far enough ahead before she followed back towards the town. Then she heard the sound of voices, a couple who were arguing at the foot of the bank, fifty yards away. The girl was wearing a scuffed leather jacket, short black skirt and the obligatory Doc Marten boots. She was sitting on the wet grass, bare mud-scraped knees drawn up to her chin. Myra thought there was something familiar about her: one of the three teenage daughters from next door perhaps, or one of the travellers who came to the school to pick up the kids. But she was hiding her face behind her hands. The man, much taller, was wearing a studded biker's jacket, grubby jeans, and he was pacing the ground between the girl and an old blue transit van, such as the travellers used, a few yards away. He was swinging his arms, shouting, though Myra could not hear what he was saying. He dropped to his knees in front of the girl, bawling at the side of her head, upper body lurching with the strength of his delivery, arms and fists held rigidly at the sides until he could contain himself no longer and he took a swipe at the top of the girl's head. And when he hit her again, with the back of his hand, the girl let her hands drop to reveal a coldly smiling face, red hair in a tight pony tail, not the hardbitten gypsy Myra had believed her to be, but her colleague, Kate.

The chilly darkening afternoon took on a watching look and Myra stood, her stomach lifting. She wondered if she should go immediately across to them, but she seemed unable to move. She looked about for help, madly wishing for anyone who might offer advice. An elderly couple with a white terrier walked no more than ten feet from Kate, but they took no notice other than to call the dog away. Further on, three men came out of the bushes, laughing, toting boxes of fishing gear. As Kate launched into a salvo of abuse at the man, whom Myra took to be David, the men paused, watching, sudden laughter inspired by some comment from one of them. This made Myra angry. Another fucked-up couple, the insoluble war of the sexes, that's all it meant to them. Hadn't they heard the war was over? Didn't they know that men and women just wanted to be friends these days? John would not have been so obtuse. It was a situation in which he would have thrived, the old John, calm and tactful, and for a moment their difficulties were forgotten and Myra wished he were here.

Feeling the stirring weight of her middle-class upbringing, her entire philosophy of civilised life – useless here in these open spaces – Myra took a few brave steps forward. Now David was picking Kate up and carrying her, one bare leg trailing, to the bank and a straight twelve-foot drop to the water. Myra froze, horrified, knowing she should call out, yet incapable of mustering a single word. Then David relented and dumped Kate on a patch of bare ground. She screeched at him, 'Fuck you, fuck you,' and scrambled back to the place where she had been sitting before, still shouting, David replying with a simultaneous barrage of indecipherable anger.

At this point something about the whole scenario struck Myra as oddly familiar, universal. She began to see it as a symbolic routine, a labyrinthine searching for some unfindable answer. In Kate's new iced smile she saw a failure of spontaneity, twists of weary aggression, old and rehearsed tolerances. This was something they did to each other. They did it all the time. Myra wondered about this rapid insight, concerned it might be no more than a product of her fear of intervening in the row. Yet it was true that she did not know the full story about these two. This was all she had to go on – David pulling Kate's arm now, she half allowing him to drag her to the van where he pushed her into the passenger seat, slamming the door on her. Then he got in himself, starting the engine, crunching the gears as he drove up the flood bank and over, the van's loose rear doors dancing open and shut as it sped away on the rough grassland.

Myra let her arms fall weakly to her sides and began the walk home, physically drained, a hole in her thoughts that could not be filled by any kind of reason. Love, hate, how easily the two coiled together, the one breeding from the other. Why did it always have to be this way? A teenage couple walked towards her, their arms around each other. Myra quickened her pace, avoiding their looks.

10

Sunday, a storm.

To Myra, its coming seemed like the arrival of old knowledge. The wind was first, high above the town, drawing the lower warmer air upwards. Moments later, the rain came in a furious flux, carrying a hail that she could feel pinging on the padded shoulders of her coat. She ran the last hundred yards to the house. By the time she had got through the door she was drenched. She put her coat on a chair in the kitchen and went upstairs for a towel to dry her hair. Walking back along the landing she stopped to watch the storm's progress through the window. A flash of lightning illuminated the detail of her hand on the glass as she leaned on the sill. The thunder followed, at first a mute distant rumble, moments later an explosion immediately overhead. The light had turned green with the rain which lulled surprisingly, only to return in an even, concerted squall, the water spilling in sheets from the roof. The clouds above the playing field were motionless, a thick purple ceiling, though Myra could see, less than a mile away, a lake of blue sky trimmed with the white cumuli of fair weather.

The rain eased and the thunder achieved a metallic, searing quality then lessened, moving on, cracking down elsewhere over York. Away to the north alarms had begun to ring in shops, a hospital, and a fire engine made its urgent wailing way along the top road arousing vague connotations of war. Myra pulled her blouse out of her skirt and undid the top buttons to dry her neck, the towel soothing against her skin. The wind sucked at a gap in the window frame, flashes of lightning still lit the landing, a tardy roll of thunder rumbled on the roof, but it was less convincing now. She went downstairs and looked through the net curtains of the lounge window. A lost hiker emerged from an alley where he had been sheltering, a map clenched between his teeth as he shuffled a backpack on to his shoulders. Children appeared in the new sunlight, and women Myra did not know came out of their front doors on their way to the off-licence, the launderette, all seeming to want to reassert themselves against nature, conceited over the way it had left them unharmed, unchanged. Myra turned back into the room, the only evidence of the storm's having existed at all being the heavy drips from a leaking gutter that caught the sill of the back door in random ones and twos.

Alex had been out since the previous afternoon, as usual, and John, in answer to an early phone call which he said was something to do with work, had gone out and still not returned. Myra did not believe him. She could hardly believe a thing he said, these days, that is, when he could actually bring himself to speak to her. Sometimes he was merely subdued, at other times he seemed on the edge of some rage he dare not let fly. Perhaps he had gone out because he couldn't face another day alone with her? Things could not go on like this.

She went into the kitchen and put the kettle on, turning the unread newspaper on the table, thinking to sit with it for half an hour before . . . Before what? In one minute flat she resurrected and discarded a string of old ideas for self-improvement – the reading of the history of York, writing for an Open University curriculum, the devising of a daily exercise routine. When she had not been working there never seemed time for such things – she had too much time, it weighed her down like a heavy blanket. But now, with work, with someone else about the house, her mind had become alert, scheming how she could fit everything in. Until these last few days. She was lonely. And John had made her so.

She thought of Sunday lunches when she had been a child, when her father was home on leave – roast beef and horseradish sauce, plum duff and custard. When had she last sat down to a Sunday lunch like that? She must visit her mother soon. It had been almost six months since the last time. But she couldn't quite face it, sure that she would be unable to hide the fact that things were so poor between her and John. The kettle bubbled up and clicked itself off. Today might be the day for confrontation with him. It was on the cards. There would never be a perfect moment for it, but the wound had to be opened and the foul matter drained away. She did not want to hurt him, she never wanted that. But she had new life now, regeneration, and she wanted to keep it that way. If only John could join her, could return from the dark days with her, recast the self, breathe new air with an optimism so deep and rich that no one else alive could possibly understand. But he seemed incapable of it, she knew, and her mind was crowded with the arguments she had against his behaviour, his coldness.

She turned the pages of the newspaper. Street riots, a kidnapping, a government crisis, the top ten PEPS. Nothing went in, but she continued to read, waiting for the passing of these jarring minutes. Gazza fit to play for England on Wednesday. Was that good? 'Jesus saves, but Gazza nets the rebound.' Graffiti. In her head. Where had she seen that? Then she heard the front door open and close. Now. It had to be now.

But it was Alex who came into the kitchen, his hair wringing, jacket soaked through, shirt front clinging to his skin like wet tissue paper.

Myra felt relieved. The appearance of another human being threw her train of thought. The confrontation was off, at least for the time being. It would probably have been a mistake anyway. Some other time, perhaps, a natural moment, unlooked for.

'So the storm caught you out too, did it?' she said.

'Brilliant,' said Alex. 'What's it look like?'

He took off his jacket and dried his face with the towel Myra had left on the table.

'Leave the wet stuff out and I'll put it in the wash.'

'It'll be OK. Besides, I want this shirt for tomorrow.'

'Of course. Work.'

'Yeah, work.' He tossed the towel aside and kicked off his shoes.

'You sound fed up with it already,' said Myra.

'Yeah, well . . .'

He wiped his nose with the back of his hand, went to feel the teapot, then came and sat at the other side of the table.

'I was about to make tea,' said Myra. 'Want some?'

'Go on, then.'

Myra fussed about with the teapot, a little light-headed with having her grey solitude so suddenly interrupted. She felt her mood lifting of its own accord and began chattering brightly about her looking forward to work in the morning, about the sense of purpose it had given her. These things came tumbling out, things she had never said to John.

'It's all right for you,' said Alex. 'You're, I don't know . . . qualified, clever.'

'I don't think that makes any difference.'

She was in control of the situation, knowing she could manipulate Alex's mood, the big young man's gloom that had hold of him. She liked Alex, he was of the world, letting himself slide with its tugs and pulls. His youth was an education to her. She hoped he would stay young, die young, to keep the bloom, the grace of spontaneity. Without thinking, she went over to him and began undoing the buttons of his shirt.

'Here. I can do this now,' she said. 'It'll be ready for morning.'

'Myra! Give over.' He laughed and pulled himself away.

'No, really. It's no problem,' said Myra, beginning to laugh herself.

'Stop it! Myra . . .'

'Come on.' She pulled the shirt down over his arms. This was something John should see. It was a lark, a fooling around he never went in for.

Then she stopped and they were facing each other. She could feel the heat on his face, smell his warm breath. And she kissed him, quickly, the action performed naturally, before thought and logic could make their puritanical interventions. He sniggered emptily and stood, looking away, trying to hide his embarrassment.

'I'm sorry,' said Myra. 'I shouldn't have done that.'

'It's OK.'

'I don't know what I was thinking of.'

'Don't apologise.'

After the last time, that night after they had been to the pub, her behaviour was inexcusable. She shook her head and leaned on the sink, looking out over the backyard wall to the playing field where a woman was throwing a ball for her dog, a woman of Myra's age, in control of her own life, of her senses, who could never be given to the foolishness of kissing a mere boy.

'I feel very stupid,' she said.

'No need for that. Where's John?'

'Out.'

'That's all right, then.'

Myra heard his two soft steps as he came up behind her. His first touch on her shoulder felt heavy, the second, about her waist, heavier. She turned to face him and he put his arms around her and pulled her to him, nuzzling her neck.

'A bit of this does no harm,' he said.

'I don't know . . .'

'Nice?' he said. 'Nice, isn't it?'

Myra closed her eyes and nodded. The touching, the warmth, the unthinkingness. This was what she wanted, a need unknown a few minutes before. Now it was so obvious. It would *save* her. She was travelling again, to the centre of her self, that room full of answers. He put his hand in her blouse but she pulled it out and led him from the kitchen, past the closed front door, nurturing the sense of decadence, half wanting John to come in at this moment. He had driven her to this. It was her way of getting her own back, and it didn't seem to matter whether he knew or not. Old thoughts, ancient sensibilities told her that this was a mistake. Yet it was a mistake she wanted to make, to lose control, be made use of. It was natural. It need not be tragic. They went up the stairs to Alex's room where he took hold of her with a look of gain, both manly and infantile.

'This once,' Myra said. 'Just this one time.'

'Right. That's how I like it too.'

With this weak rule established Myra let herself go, pulling at his clothes, chasing her need of him, only fleetingly sure of its existence. Her head had nothing to do with this, she must keep it quiet, be an animal. She salivated a little at the touch of his skin and hair, and there was a spiced urgency behind the sternum, in her breasts as she undressed herself. These things were going on in her body. She was her body, that's all she needed to be. Then they were both naked and an old gorgeous feeling rose up to her stomach. Alex smiled with a charming coyness, his prick, that silly appurtenance, standing to attention. He was taller than John, taller than her, which made her feel desirable. She took hold of his prick, feeling its knobbled underside with her fingertips, tracing the vessels and contours along its length. Such a ridiculous shape! She smiled, a smile of the body, taking his inexpert fingers and guiding them where she wanted them to be while he kissed her mouth, her breasts.

Myra drew him on to the bed and eased him into her, his entry slow and hesitant, clumsily teasing. This made her want to laugh, but she was careful not to. Then he was fully inside her and she was rediscovering the sweet tension of arousal, looking for its release as she sought to make his efforts smoother and reciprocal. She was holding him hard, licking the young skin that still smelled of the rain. This was wrong. And it was right. Either way, it didn't matter. Nice. That was what he said it should be. Nice. In her schooldays that had been a forbidden word. It has no meaning, the teacher would say. It's a childish word. Silly. But maybe it could be the word for this, this gift from God. Nice. It said it all.

But it was over too soon. Alex rolled away. He had another identity now. She did not know who he was. She pulled a sheet around her. This had been neither right nor wrong. Nor satisfying. It had only been in her mind after all. The body had stirred but the earth had not moved, remaining as unyielding as ever beneath her. It was something she had done, that was all. It would be forgotten – she was forgetting already, wanting to get away from Alex at the first seemly moment.

He was lying at her side, red-faced and grinning. He pulled his legs up and slapped his knees.

'Roger,' he said.

'What?'

'Roger the lodger. Me, the lodger. Rogering for the purposes of.'

And he laughed loudly, pleased with himself.

At Little Pawnton, even the local farmers had to agree that it was one of the best summers for years. Myra and John explored the hills without a map, looking for the best possible views, coming across a lake, its water running brown with the residues of an old iron working, finding both picturesque cottages and derelict stone farms in the middle of nowhere.

On weekdays Myra made friends with a woman at the opposite end of their row whose name was Julie. She was separated and had a two-year-old son. Myra found her a capable and likeable character and on alternate weekends they began babysitting for each other, Julie having formed an attachment with a doctor from Runcorn who she privately hoped might take her away from the quiet of the countryside. Laura hated the arrangement, thinking herself too mature to be closeted with the younger child. And when she came back she would be full of stories about his incessant crying and his constantly wanting to be picked up.

On their night out, Myra and John went no further than the first of the village pubs, The Feathers, an old coaching house with shiny stone floors and a landlord who, once he got to trust people, would lock the doors at closing time and let the regulars carry on until early in the morning. When he invited them to stay back for one of these sessions, John was delighted, taking it as further progress in their being accepted in the village. 'That's it. We're in. Country folk now, lass, that's us.' But they only stayed an hour, John surpassing his limited tolerance of alcohol and falling asleep, much to the amusement of Chuck and some of the other men in the bar.

In early August John's sister, Connie, who lived at the other side of Manchester, invited them to join her and her husband on a trip to the States. John had three weeks' holiday coming up, but he was tired and he just wanted to spend the time at their new home. Myra agreed. Life had become so equable, so new, she almost feared missing any of it. A holiday? There seemed no point. Unlike the younger Julie and her disaffection for the village, Myra's feelings lay at the other end of the axis. Life had begun to seem like one long holiday, these days. And to think it could never continue that way, she thought, would have been neurotic . . .

On Monday, Alex was up before anyone else for the first time since his arrival at the house. Myra could hear him downstairs, opening kitchen cupboards, looking for something and grumbling when he could not find it. Then she heard the rasp of his cigarette lighter and the boiling of the kettle.

She turned over and looked at John, asleep with his back to her. The hair on his back extended into a small blond delta between his shoulders. One bare knee was sticking out from under the duvet he had crumpled up to his chest. He had arrived home late the previous night self-absorbed, but not surly. He suspected nothing about her and Alex, Myra knew that. And a few hours' revision of the incident had led her to believe that, for all that such a thing had once been John's mad suggestion, he should never know what had happened. It would destroy him. Besides, it was already a distant event in Myra's mind, sealed in a little box, a folly of her own making, a waywardness that might somehow, in the sump of their unspoken dealings with each other, solve a few problems. She had taken a revenge of sorts, and John knew nothing about it.

Myra slipped out of bed, put on her dressing-gown and went downstairs. Alex was pacing the kitchen floor, the air sickly with the cheap tobacco he used.

'Well, best be off.' He stared hard at the clock on the wall. 'Need to put on a good show. First impressions and that.'

He was wearing his leather bomber and jeans, and the creased tie, the only one he seemed to possess.

'I could give you a lift, if you can hang on for half an hour.'

'No,' he said sharply. 'I can make my own way.'

'Right, well, good luck.' She smiled, carefully. 'Hope it all goes well for you.'

'Yeah. Right.'

He stubbed out the latest cigarette, dropping the butt among the four that were already in the ashtray, giving the clock one last serious look.

'See you later, then.'

'Yes. Bye, Alex.'

And he was gone, with nothing revealed of his thoughts about the previous afternoon. He was being more sensible than Myra dared have hoped, perhaps dismissing it all, delightfully, as no more than a passing incident. He was young. It was the sort of thing young men dreamed of, a gilt-edged sexual opportunity that he might recount to his mates in the pub. Got it on a plate, she imagined him saying. On a fucking plate.

She made tea and took a cup up for John, finding him already awake.

'Late again.' He yawned and sat up. 'Someone will be having words with me.'

'I've said it before, you work hard enough. What about yesterday?' said Myra, as she searched the wardrobe for her clothes.

'Right, yesterday.'

Myra slipped off the dressing-gown and her nightie. She turned to find John looking at her. She smiled, unusually embarrassed. What was he looking at? Was her body betraying her? Was there some aura of guilt lingering about her skin, her face? She put the dressing-gown back on and put her clothes over her arm to go to the bathroom.

'Yesterday,' he said, pensively.

'What about it?' Her heart failed a little.

'In the afternoon, on my way back, I called in to see the old man. After the last time I thought, you know, it might be better if I went alone, toughed it out, so to speak. I thought it might make things easier. I had this feeling that I wanted to talk to him, even if he couldn't understand a thing I was saying. I didn't think it could do any harm.'

'And did it?' said Myra, hiding her relief.

'No.' He bit his top lip. 'Anyway, I . . . There's something else.'

'Oh?'

'The nurse. New woman, not seen her before. She told me he's been running a temperature the last few days. Chest infection, probably. Anyway, he was in bed. More on fuller's earth than this. Must be the antibiotics they're using.'

'They're treating him there?'

'Yes. They use a local GP or something. Funny, I always thought the next of kin got a say in things like this. Still . . .' He breathed out, softly. 'It's what I'd have wanted them to do, if they'd asked. Treat him, I mean.'

'They should have rung and let you know.'

'She said they'd meant to.'

Myra sat down on the edge of the bed and took his hands between hers.

'I'm sorry.'

He shrugged. 'Nothing to be done, I'm afraid. I'll just have to be ready for, you know . . . We could do without it, I think.'

'We'll manage.'

'Will we? Oh, I know I've been a bit glum lately. I'm just trying to square things in my head. I want to be like you. You're so practical. Maybe it's because you're a woman. They're a sharper lot than men, these days anyway. You're so clear-headed. It's like you've got, I don't know . . . Night vision. It's as if you can see in the dark. With me, getting through a day's like trying to claw through concrete.' He put his arms around her, kissed her forehead, drew breath between his teeth. 'It seems so easy for you.'

'Does it?' Myra rested her head on his shoulder, and looked away through the window, lost for words.

A quarter moon was hanging in the east, the air holding a dampness, a reserve about itself as if it might rapidly materialise into a blanket of cloud. It was that time of year, thought Myra, when the weather became wilful, assuming control in earthly matters. Not winter, not yet. But soon.

As she pulled into the school car-park the only other figure around was a solitary boy in the playground. He was holding his bag by the straps, kicking it to make it spin. He was far too early, dumped there, no doubt, by busy parents off to do whatever they did in the rushing, time-obsessed world. As she got out of the car, she saw Kate walking in through the school's pedestrian entrance. Myra shouted a cheerful hello, but Kate just hunched her shoulders and went inside. She locked the car and went in through the main double doors, following the trail of her colleague's perfume along the corridor to Rowena's office.

It was the first time Myra had seen her since that day by the river, and for a moment the memory felt unreliable, thrown by the black Jaeger suit and prim blouse Kate was wearing. But the haughty toss of the head, her slight shape, reaffirmed Myra's identification of her. In truth, she had half forgotten the incident, though it was returning now, uncomfortably clear, and Myra found herself looking for signs of damage about Kate's pale face and neck. She wondered if Kate had actually seen her watching the display she and her boyfriend had given. She was making herself overtly busy, flicking through files of teaching aids, acknowledging Myra's presence with no more than a barely audible 'Mmm'. Myra went to the quiet room to put the kettle on for the customary quick coffees they all had before work.

In a deliberate show of deference, more importantly to confound Kate's iciness, Myra made a drink for her as well and, with the first children running into the cloakroom, she went back to the office with it. Rowena had arrived, in her heavy grey coat, papers under one arm, her other arm about Kate's shoulder, patting her as she went. She raised her palm indicating to Myra that she might leave them alone. Myra, without stopping, turned on her heels and went back to the quiet room. There, she found Andrew spooning his usual three sugars into a mug of black coffee.

'Problems,' said Myra.

'Tell me something new,' he said, burning his lips on his drink.

'It's Kate. She's upset about something.'

'Can't think of a day when she wasn't. I shouldn't worry about it.'

'Really?'

'Oh, sure. Just remember we don't take exception to it. We get on. We do our little bit and we ignore it. Best way.'

'But why? What gets into her?'

'Boyfriends usually,' he said, drily. 'Or not, as the case may be.'

He seemed about to add to his remark when a fair-haired girl from his class ran into the room. She had a bright red toy treasure chest which she held up for Andrew to see.

'Look,' she said, proudly. 'Dad got me it from Saudi.'

Andrew took the chest and held it up, inspecting it with one eye in mocking imitation of a jewellery expert.

'That's lovely, Sara. Are you going to show it to the others?'

'No. I just wanted you to see it, that's all.'

'Oh, right. And would you like me to keep it in my desk till home time?'

'Yes, I would.' She turned to Myra. 'It's valuable, you know.'

'Well, I'd better look after it then, hadn't I?' Andrew said.

The girl looked doubtfully at her possession then ran out of the room. Andrew put the chest down, eyeing it impassively.

'They used to bring the things they'd made – models, pictures, you know. Now it's just what they've been able to acquire. Worries me sometimes. Sickens me a bit. And the stuff they have. Do you know, I found one of them, Tom, with a sponge ball thing the other day. He said it was a "stress ball". Christ, he's six years old.'

Myra studied him carefully – long-chinned, bristle-haired, body a little too small for the head. He was an ungainly runner, as she had noticed when he took the kids for the football practice he hated. He would be no more than twenty-five, but he looked older, careworn. Where had he picked up this scepticism about children? She wanted him to forget his musings, to urge him on about Kate, the need for information fuelled as, through the open door, they both saw Rowena guiding their distraught colleague to an empty office near the main doors. Andrew tutted.

Emboldened by his disapproval, Myra said, 'I saw her the other day, Kate.'

'Did you?'

'With her boyfriend. Or at least I assume it was him. They were arguing.'

'Doesn't surprise me.'

'And he hit her. It looked as if it could get very ugly.'

'It'd not be the first time. I think she rather gets a kick out of that sort of thing.'

'Oh, come on.'

'No, it's true. She's complex, our Katie. Anyway,' he said, rinsing his cup at the sink, 'you're only here till the end of term. Then you'll be out of it. Best not get involved, yes? Life'll be much simpler for you.'

Myra nodded, sensing the wisdom of his words, the potential folly of her own inquisitiveness.

The day started twenty minutes late with the children, unled by time, running wild in the corridors. Andrew, increasingly annoyed, went at last to find Rowena, returning a minute later, saying wearily that he would be taking assembly and they'd better get on with it now.

Afterwards Myra, detecting the anarchy that the break in routine had inspired in the children, set them easy, achievable tasks. As an *ad hoc* part of the Water Project she gave one group of six – the tardiest learners in her charge – the simple job of drawing the storm they had seen yesterday. After half an hour, four of them had produced predictable felt-tipped images of each other in wellington boots, splashing through puddles, their parents holding enormous umbrellas. The other two, both travellers' kids, had a theme of their own, with one picture of a horse running, the other of it lying on its back, stick legs upturned to yellow zigzags in the sky. One of their horses, they clamoured to explain, attracting embellishing comments from the travellers in other groups, had been startled by the thunder and had bolted, breaking its neck against a wall.

It was two o'clock when Myra returned home, entering the house and noticing its warmth and an occupant she had not expected.

Alex was in the lounge, sprawled across the sofa, watching television. On the floor beside him was the ashtray and an open packet of Benson and Hedges. He was still wearing the clothes he had gone out in that morning.

'Didn't expect you.' Her voice betrayed a little irritation. She had been hoping for a couple of hours alone, doing nothing more strenuous than flicking through the pages of a magazine, perhaps having a nap on the sofa. 'Early finish?'

'Flexi-time,' he said, not taking his eyes off the screen. 'Nothing on this afternoon. Guy, the bloke I was with, said I might as well go home. So, here I am. Satisfied?'

'Sorry. I was only asking.'

'You shouldn't. You're not my folks.'

Myra shrugged. Not his folks. How the tables had turned, how different things had been just twenty-four hours ago. Now he was guilty about something, touchy with the matriarchal figure he was taking Myra for. She went through to the kitchen, her breathing laboured by her tiredness and his mild threat of confrontation. Then he came up behind her.

He was pacing the floor, smiling oddly, sourly, the way he did when something was on his mind.

'You know, I've been thinking,' he said, scanning the ceiling. 'This house.'

'What about it?'

'All these rooms. Two empty on the landing. Bet there's at least two more in the attic. In fact, I know there is. I looked.'

'Did you?' said Myra, unhappy with the idea of him prowling about the place when they were not there.

'Yeah. And I was thinking you ought to think about letting them all off, not just my room. Get students in. You could get two or three to the bigger rooms. They're not fussy.'

'Is that right?'

'Sure it is. Why not do it? There's a fortune to be made. Right here, under your own roof.'

Myra's empty stomach rolled. Her legs were aching and the tiny corns on each of her little toes were sore. She sat at the table, resting her hands on its surface. His suggestion aroused uncomfortable feelings. He was getting too close, being presumptuous. She wondered if he had walked out on the job. That would mean another face-to-face over the money he owed them. John's idea that he should help about the place had begun that evening with the washing-up and ended the next afternoon with a sulky ten minutes spent clearing a few bits of wood to the side of the yard before he went out. And then there had been yesterday . . .

'The house isn't ours to let.'

'I could run it for you. You could still go to work. Two incomes. How about that?'

'You're not listening, Alex. I said, the house doesn't belong to us. We can't just up and do a thing like that.'

'Why not? I'm here, aren't I?'

'The house belongs to John's father. He let us have it . . .' She paused, Bill's ghost somewhere in the walls, watching, the ghost of a man still alive. 'He let us have it when things became difficult for us. It's still his property.'

'So what's the odds? Sublet. Cut him in on the profits. Bet he wouldn't say no to that.'

'It can't be done. Anyway, he's ill. Maybe one day we'll have to sell the place to raise the money to look after him. And besides,' she went on, feeling faint with tension, 'I wouldn't want a house full of strangers. We have one boarder. That's you and it's enough. So forget it. All right?'

Alex was standing at her side, big hands planted on a chair back, boring into her skull with his eyes, those sharp blue eyes where his thwarted plans were fermenting to anger. It unnerved Myra, making her feel fragile.

'That's it, is it? That's all you've got to say?'

'Yes.'

'Well, thanks, Myra. Thanks a whole bloody bunch.'

'I'm sorry.'

'Course you are. You've made me look a right prick, do you know that?'

'I haven't. And I don't mean to upset you.'

'No. Bloody sure you don't. I'm all right when you want something, aren't I? Like yesterday. Right? Then when it's my turn, when I want you to do something for me . . . Ahh, fuck you, Myra. Fuck you.'

He turned and left the room, the house, slamming the front door, leaving his voice on the air, an echo of all the male indignation she had suffered down the years – none from her father, nor from John, curiously: his was all self-inflicted. But there had been a deal from the boyfriends she had discarded in her youth, from holier-than-thou civil rights protesters she could not agree with, from the misogynist headmaster at her last school in Manchester.

She looked up out of the window at the afternoon clouds, a powdery mass above the skyline of rooftops and bare trees, the sun hiding itself prudishly away. Perhaps it is winter, she thought. Perhaps it has been here a while.

A rash of red 'Sale' signs appeared in shop windows and more homely handwritten notices for carol services were posted outside the town's churches. Christmas was coming to York. In Parliament Street a fun-fair was being erected, hammers tapping in a straddling tempo, challenging the jigs of a lone violinist in the doorway of Marks and Spencer. Children clutched parents' hands, happily infected with the growing fever of the coming season. And the tourists still came, Americans in tartan trousers and berets, Geordies with camcorders filming the Minster, stealing the history. To Myra's eyes the Europeans all seemed to walk in the same fashion, relaxed but hesitant, their expressions a little flustered as if they could not properly absorb the grandeur of the place. Stone to flesh – they could not quite get it into their skins.

After the half-term holiday, the heating was turned up full at the school, bringing a sweet fragrance from the fresh timber floors. Here, Christmas was already a big issue. There were parents to be cajoled into the making of costumes for the nativity play, carols to be taught and rehearsed. But when Myra tried to get the kids to learn the words of 'O Come All Ye Faithful', her main problem was in getting the hysterical class not to sing the words of a TV jingle which was using the tune to advertise car exhausts. The work required extra hours which Myra offered to do freely, three afternoons a week, if necessary. Rowena was glad to accept, saying she would see she got the time back, though Myra did not see how this could happen since her contract had less than four weeks to run. Kate said as much, adding waspishly that she would not give one more minute of her time than she was being paid for.

Away from work, Myra had not given the season much thought. John had not mentioned it at all, though he usually looked forward to Christmas. Things were better between them now and a little effort on both their parts might make it worthwhile, with a new year to look forward to, then spring, then . . . she was still unsure. The state of Bill's health was a central concern. For the moment he was holding his own, but a change for the worse would certainly sour any celebrations they might plan. And Myra did not want good intentions going to waste.

She decided against pushing through the crowds in The Shambles and turned back into the market with its stalls of fruit and fish, polythene-wrapped clothing, the cold air alive with the ribald talk of the traders. And her thoughts turned to Alex. He had not been around for the last four days, sleeping at the house just once, as far as Myra knew. She still had no regrets about having had sex with him. It was the first time she had been unfaithful to John, and if ever the idea had crossed her mind before she imagined such an act would leave her tainted, an adultress – a word that suddenly came to mind bearing a certain graphic appeal. It meant she had needs, that she was alive and human. But fumbling around with Alex again was a charmless idea. It had been silly, such a loveless event, and she needed love. And warmth, and food, and shelter – Maslow's Hierarchy of Needs. Where had she learned about that?

She fully expected Alex to be gone soon, after the

weekend perhaps. He owed more than two weeks' money and Myra was sure he would not be able to find it. He was that sort of creature, impulsive with money, throwing it at the immediate needs of the senses. If he did come up with it, all well and good, though Myra was half hoping he wouldn't, sensing that he was becoming an irritation to John, their relationship dying a predictable death. Alex had too much life about him. John could not compete.

The walk back by the river induced a lazy mood, the buzz of the town, her thoughts about Christmas, all behind her somewhere. In the Museum Gardens a peacock screeched and in the dying light a groundsman was shovelling leaves into an orange covered trailer. There was a sharpness in the air that might bring a night frost, the first of winter, and a hard breeze was making the litter rattle on the cobbles. Myra shuddered and made her way up the steps.

When she reached the street she stopped, her stomach lifting. Their door was half open and her first thought was that Alex might be in there, helping himself to a few of their belongings as well as his own, before disappearing into the night. Then she noticed John's car further up the street, parked at a slight angle to the kerb. She breathed deeply and went inside, closing the door firmly to announce her arrival.

John was in the lounge, pacing the floor, holding a cigarette from which he took two short drags before putting it out.

'Afternoon off?' said Myra, shaking herself out of her coat.

'No.' He closed his eyes and rubbed his forehead. 'Look, Myra, are you busy right now?'

'No. Why?'

'I'd like to go out. To the home.'

'Had we planned to go this afternoon?' Myra asked, knowing they had made no such arrangement.

'No. It's, well, they rang me.'

'Oh. I see.' She folded the coat over her arm, slowly. John's lips moved as if he was rehearsing something he wanted to say. 'You mean he's worse?'

'Yes. Yes, I do,' he said, opening his eyes wide, wringing his fingers. 'Yes,' again. 'I have to go. Would you mind coming with me?'

'No. Of course not. We'll go now, if you like.'

It was a young man who showed them up to Bill's room, a slim smooth type with gelled-back hair, a floral shirt, trousers with front pleats. Narcissistic, thought Myra. She had not seen him before, though John seemed to know him. At a guess he could have been the owner's son, leading them up the stairs with a comfortable air, rattling keys, tapping at the walls, thinking perhaps of the value of the building when the backside had fallen out of the private care market. He took them along the landing where odours of the residents' tea still lingered, onion, egg, a meal taken at four o'clock every day, everyone in bed for nine. Like children, Myra thought. The young man went straight into Bill's room, forgoing the quaint knock that Shirley went in for.

The only light came from a small lamp in the corner, and from the television which was on with the volume turned down. Bill was in bed, sleeping, cheeks ruddy beneath the silver shimmer of beard, white flecks of spittle in the corners of his mouth, his forehead yellow and shiny. He had lost weight and was now perhaps only half the man, literally, that Myra had once known. It was a shock to her. He looked like the victim of an accident, and Myra felt a flush of anger that free-floated against the young man, as if it had been his fault and he had done nothing to help Bill.

'Hello, Dad,' said John, looking somewhere to the far side of his father.

The young man picked up a temperature chart from the end of the bed, pouting as he flipped over the pages. Play-acting, thought Myra, tactless, the body in the bed no more than a financial unit to him.

'Still high. Just the same, really.' He looked at Bill with at least a glimmer of duty, Myra thought. He replaced the chart by feeling for its hook as he spoke. 'Dr Greenaway came this afternoon. It was him who suggested I get in touch with you.'

John nodded, pale and reduced.

'Is he eating?' asked Myra.

'Well, bits. Not much. I could have his tea sent up and you can try him with it, if you like.'

'No,' John said, quietly. 'I don't think so.'

Myra frowned at him.

'Maybe we could try him with a little, if he wakes up,' she said. 'There'd be no harm in that, surely.'

John scratched his ear and breathed out fully. Myra caught the young man's eye and nodded. He seemed more cautious now, aware of the deep water of John's concern. He returned Myra's nod and left the room.

'There was no need for that,' said John. 'It's their job. It doesn't seem right.'

'Tosh. I'll do it. Anyway, he looks too out of it to want anything.'

'So why bother?'

'Because we should.'

Myra knew she ought not be so hard on him, but she could not hide her annoyance. She switched off the television and brought the stool to the side of the bed. John was being foolish, over-reacting. It wasn't like him, at least not like the considerate man she had once known. What was he really afraid of? The intimacy of feeding his own father? The fact that he might not really have any feelings for him? She sat with her back to John, watching his father,

listening to his shallow breath. A minute later they heard a
female yelp and the laughter of the young man somewhere
along the landing. Footsteps followed, a gentle knock at the
door, and a girl no more than fourteen years old entered.
She was carrying a bowl of soup, a slice of white bread,
and a feeding mug half filled with tea. She set the things
down by the television on the chest of drawers.

'You break up the bread and put it in,' she said, as if
repeating some mundane instruction she had been given
by way of training. 'But not the crusts. They can choke
on those.'

'Thank you,' said Myra.

The girl went back towards the door then stopped,
looking dreamily at Bill.

'Sad, isn't it? My aunt was like that. Last year. Upset the
whole family. Anyway . . .' She tilted her head to one side,
still looking at Bill. 'If you want any help, just call.'

'We will,' said Myra, her impatience abating. She was
thinking about the other residents, the more alert ones,
wondering how they coped with such a snip of a girl, how
easily one could be defeated by the mores and routines of
an institution like this. What would Myra be like in such
a place? An awkward old hag? Or a little lamb, happy to
comply with whatever rules made life easier? She would
have liked to think she could put up a fight, but when
they owned you, your body, owned all of your time, the
most powerful spirit must eventually be broken.

The girl left the room, closing the door with a bang that
made Bill stir and open his rheumy eyes. He looked up,
then to his side, offering a quivering half-smile when he
saw John.

'Look,' said Myra. 'He recognises you.'

'No, he doesn't.'

'Why shouldn't he? They're supposed to remember some
things.'

Bill attempted to lift his hand under the bedcovers, murmuring a soft 'ah' and coughing unproductively.

'Maybe we should try and sit him up,' said Myra.

'No.'

'Oh, come on. It's good for a bad chest. He shouldn't be lying low like that.'

Myra leaned over the old man and put her hands under his armpits, managing to heave him up a few inches on the pillows until his 'ahs' came again and he shouted a loud 'Hey!' in protest.

'Myra . . .'

'It's all right.' She pulled the covers up to Bill's chin.

'Please,' said John. He came over and took hold of her shoulders. 'I can't stand it. Please leave him alone.' And he squeezed her hands tight between his.

On the way back, John was quiet, subdued as the dark country road, brightening only when they reached the rows of street lights on the outskirts of town.

'I'm sorry,' he said. 'Back there. Maybe I go over the top a bit. I'm too sensitive, I know, but it's just so hard to take, coming on top of everything else like this.'

'I understand,' said Myra, who was questioning her own attitude, thinking herself meddlesome. She felt a little ashamed, sad for John, realising, not for the first time, that she might be underestimating the depth and complexity of his feelings for his father.

John sighed.

'And what I said that night in bed. About my not minding if you wanted, you know . . . I don't know why I said that. Stupid. I didn't mean it. I'm sorry.'

The colour swam into Myra's cheeks.

'It doesn't matter. I knew you didn't mean it. Forget about it.'

He pulled off the bypass on to a brief stretch of unlit road, the big bare hawthorns on either side brought closer by the headlights.

'I was thinking,' he said. 'It being the weekend and all that. I thought I might go and see Connie. Maybe stay tomorrow night, see if she wants to come through here for a few days. She hasn't been yet, and I know she'd want to.'

'Good idea. She could be a big help to you.' Myra was relieved that he had changed the subject.

'It's just, I don't know . . . Running away. I feel as if I'd be running away.'

'Don't. I'll be here if anything happens. Or would you like me to come with you?'

'No. I think I'd rather like to go alone.'

The unlit road gave way to a suburban residential estate, the orange-lit bends in the streets inviting the way to the city centre.

'It would mean you going near the old place,' said Myra, knowing it had to be mentioned, its name unutterable.

'I can make a detour. Anyway, why should I be frightened of it? There's nothing to be frightened of, you've said it yourself, often.'

Myra shifted in her seat, looking ahead at the next broad road that led into town, at an illuminated advert for Wispa bars in a bus-shelter, the queue in a chip shop, the floodlit city walls ahead. Home. The word flipped up in her mind. This was home now, the last place, the village, only transiently recalled these days, like a historical date, fudged in the memory.

'You will be all right, won't you?' She looked down at the sill of the dashboard, at the knees of her brushed denim jeans.

'I think so.'

'You only think so?'

'OK, I'm sure. Why shouldn't I be all right? Christ, I'm a grown man, Myra.' He laughed, but emptily.

After he had cleared the tree, taking the logs through the village in a wheelbarrow, Danny came to the house each day that week. He would turn up at odd hours, once arriving just before dusk, as if he had only belatedly remembered to put in an appearance. While he put plenty of effort into clearing the garden, scything the weeds, flattening an old compost heap, Myra had doubts about him. They were helping him out, that was true, but he was part of the village and she did not want it so close, here, on her own territory. It seemed important to keep this new world at a slight remove, to be able to dictate the terms for dealing with it.

Laura came to anticipate Danny's arrival as part of a new and permanent routine. Myra stressed to her that they were only using him for this one week, but the child refused to accept this, taking a shine to the lad, though he didn't seem to like her hanging around while he worked. On the Friday afternoon Myra stood behind the open kitchen door, eavesdropping on their conversation.

'Do you have a job?' Laura asked.

'No. Not really. I do this, that's all.'

'Do you drink like my Mum and Dad? Do you go to the pub?'

'Don't bother.'

'Well, then . . .' She put her hands on her hips, exasperated by his limited replies. 'Have you got any brothers and sisters?'

'I might have.'

On Saturday morning he came again and John prompted him about the matter of payment, asking the number of hours he had put in. Danny shrugged. 'Don't know. Every day. I've been here every day.'

'All day, every day?'

Danny shrugged again, smiling.

'Well, let me see . . .'

John calculated the number of hours to be some way in excess of Myra's estimation, multiplying the lot by three pounds fifty, which she thought unwisely generous – word might get round that they were a soft touch, easy prey for anyone else in the village. She took John aside and expressed her concern, but he would have none of it, returning to the satisfied Danny, telling him where he wanted a fence putting to divide the garden into more manageable sections. Then he took the boy to a garden centre for the panels and posts. Myra thought John could easily have done the job himself, but he dismissed the idea, citing his hours at the office and the need to get the job done before winter.

Over the next few months Danny was there almost every weekday, climbing the back wall, starting work without ever announcing his arrival. When John took his holiday, he helped him with the creation of a vegetable patch, the turfing of new lawns, the erection of a shed and a gazebo at the far end of the garden. Myra was not sure about all this – it was as if John was inventing work for him. But he reassured her of its necessity, of the value it lent to the property. And he liked the boy. Myra told herself that it didn't matter, that they were becoming part of the local scene, doing their bit to help. And he was a pleasant lad, in his quiet way, showing it unexpectedly sometimes, such as when he had been shooting on the moors and turned up late one evening with a rabbit and a pheasant for them. Myra took them from him with the suspicion that he knew they would not know what to do with them. Laura took one look at the bloodied rabbit and began to cry. Myra wrapped them in newspaper and put them outside until John came home. He could only laugh over the gift, and when they had put Laura to bed he buried them in a deep hole beyond the far garden wall . . .

The next morning John seemed less sure about wanting to go to Connie's. While Myra packed a small bag for him he showered and dressed. He came down the stairs slowly, buttoning his shirt, preoccupied the way he was when there were problems at work. His expression was dull, resigned like that of a sportsman obliged to play out a game he was certain to lose.

'You don't have to go,' said Myra. 'It could wait. Perhaps Connie could just come over here?'

'No. I could use the break. Really. I haven't seen her in ages. It'll be nice. Besides, I've already told her to expect me.'

The second time he had said that. He claimed to have phoned the previous night, when Myra had gone to bed, but she had heard no sound of conversation downstairs. She also felt sure Connie's first instinct would have been to come and see Bill for herself. She was seven years older than John, with two grown-up children, and it would have been no great upheaval for her to make the trip. Myra also knew she would have appreciated the strains she and John had been under this last year, and the difficulty that Bill's deterioration might contribute to the situation.

Myra followed John into the street.

'It'll be a couple of nights or so,' said John, lowering the boot of the car. He looked more certain of himself in the daylight, now that he was on the move, and he managed a warm smile. 'I'll ring the office if I'm going to be late back. They won't mind. And I'll ring you tomorrow.'

He embraced Myra lightly, kissed her, and she watched the car all the way to the end of the street where it turned into the Saturday morning traffic filing along the top road.

The house was empty now. Alex had still not been back and she checked his room, finding jeans strewn on the floor, the holdall crumpled and empty. The clutter was everywhere, a mess that no longer seemed quaint. It was an informative moment, linking Myra with a younger self, the woman who had once taken such pride in building a home. She had been organised then, at a lifetime's peak of efficiency. And she wanted that control back. If she and John could get things worked out, she would find that power again. Perhaps after Bill had died – she recognised a secret guilty hope that he might soon be released from his pains – they could find a place of their own, reinvent both of their lives. And for the first time she saw her own efforts in this respect as selfish, her insistence on happiness excluding John, her progress a cause of his introspection. In these first few minutes of his being away from her, Myra resolved to make things better, for him, for them both.

She began stripping the bed with the idea of tidying the whole room and preparing the box room for Connie in case she decided to come back with John. After the pressures of the week, the prospect of a full day of mind-emptying physical activity pleased Myra enormously.

Within twenty minutes the room had resumed its old look, still tainted by Alex's occupation, but half-decent now, a partially reclaimed domain. She opened the window to let out the fug of Alex's socks and cigarettes and the room was filled with lively cold air from the brightening day outside. She had put all the dirty clothing she could find in the linen basket on the landing with the aim of washing it that morning and replacing it neatly in the holdall, a gesture which Alex could take any way he wanted.

She put the basket at the top of the stairs and returned for one last look round the room. All seemed well, the room's symmetrical lines re-established save for the holdall by the chair. Myra picked it up and straightened it, seeing a small brown triangle poking out of its side pocket. A wallet. At first she thought merely to push it inside and zip up the pocket, but a little mischief was in her, and she took the thing out and opened it.

All it contained was an expired membership card for the Skylight Nirvana Club in Hackney and a clipping from a page of a London freebie advertiser. It was .part of a roundup of local news, dated 30th January this year. The headline read: QUICK THINKING HERO SAVES BOY, 8, FROM ICE.

'Police have praised the actions of an Islington man who rescued a boy from almost certain death on the ice of Peeker Pond in Essex Park.

'Alexander Harrison, 17,' (seventeen!) 'a market dealer of Praetoria Gardens, was passing the locally known play area when he saw eight-year-old Tam Correy, who had been playing on the pond with friends, slip through the ice. Fast-thinking Mr Harrison dragged a ladder from a nearby workman's shed to get to the boy whose frantic efforts to stay afloat had virtually exhausted him.

'After Tam had been taken to hospital suffering from shock and hypothermia, Mr Harrison received unreserved praise from the boy's mother.

' "He's a hero," said Mrs Edith Correy, a cashier at an amusement arcade who had been working at the time of the incident. "I can't thank him enough."

' "It was nothing," Mr Harrison said modestly. "No more than any man would have done."

'*A police spokesman added to the comments about Mr Harrison's bravery with a warning that with the current cold spell, children must be strongly cautioned about the dangers of playing near frozen waterways.*'

Myra carefully replaced the clipping and pushed the wallet deep into the holdall pocket. Seventeen! She had been to bed with a boy, someone who could still have been at school. And a hero into the bargain. She smiled, feeling her ribs sinking as if a space had opened up inside her. Then she set about the work she planned for the day.

By mid-afternoon her efforts were complete. She had done the washing, Hoovered in every room downstairs, and the kitchen was spotless. She walked about the place, confidence in every movement, pride taken in the control she had achieved over the house. In the lounge she sat down on the sofa, tired, almost excessively pleased with herself. She closed her eyes for a few moments, then fell into a deep unexpected sleep.

When she woke, it was to find that the day had gone and the room was lit only by the lights from the street. The heating had burned merrily on, the even hum of the pump in the airing cupboard being the only sound she could hear. It had made the air dry, and the whole house would be oppressively and expensively warm. Then she noticed the light was on in the hall and there was someone sitting in the armchair. She sat upright, startled.

'Thought I'd best not disturb you,' Alex said, turning on the lamp at his side. 'You were well away.'

'Yes,' said Myra, rubbing her face, her thoughts collecting. 'How long have you been here?'

He lit a roll-up and eased himself deeper in the chair. 'Been in a while. Bathed, changed, ready for the evening. Saturday night, Myra, best night of the week. My room looks nice, by the way. Thanks.'

'Where have you been anyway?' Her mouth was dry and she regretted the nap. Tonight she would have difficulty in getting to sleep.

'Out and about, earning a crust. Had a bit of luck, as it happens.'

'What sort of luck?'

'Bit of business, that's all. I can pay you some of what I owe. Fifty now. More to come. Should have it by Thursday. Yeah,' he said, in serious reflection, blowing smoke at the ceiling. 'Thursday.'

He was wearing his faded black cords and an old denim shirt, the only clean clothes left in his room. Myra remembered the wallet. He looked a lot older than a teenager. She wondered if the clipping had not been about him, but someone with the same name.

'Thing is,' he said, sitting up to tap his cigarette in the ashtray, 'I fancied a bit of a celebration. Up the town. And I was wondering if you fancied coming. John, as well. I've decided I quite like him, you know.'

'He's not here at the moment.' She pointedly retained the truth about where John had gone.

'So? There's still you, isn't there? What about it? Night on the tiles, somewhere classy? Let your hair down a bit, teacher. Nothing wrong with that. Nothing wrong with being friends, is there, no obligations attached?'

Myra smiled, fully awake now, her head registering the first tightness of a headache. Out. It was Alex's answer to everything. Out was a nightly invitation to a party he could never resist. It was what he lived for, this out.

'Oh, I don't know.' She forced a yawn. She did not want to go.

'Indian first. Then a place I know, top notch. It's settled.'

'Is it? What about your friends? Why not go with them?'

'I don't have to be with them all the time, do I? Besides,

after the other day, you know, when I was going on a bit about the house, well . . . I was out of order. And I thought I could make it up to you. That's all right, isn't it?'

Myra did not know how to put him off. The space between them was too small. She wanted to say no, but she couldn't bring herself to, could not summon the rudeness needed. He knew this, he was using her politeness against her. He had every advantage. And he was bigger than her. For some reason, more subtle than physics, this seemed to matter.

'You're coming,' he said. 'Get your glad rags on. Night's not getting any younger.'

Myra thought of the silent telephone in the hall. John would not ring tonight, though the nursing home might. Yet how could anyone be expected to wait twenty-four hours a day for a call that might not come for weeks, months even? And the evening before her offered only sleeplessness. A few hours out could not be so awful, surely? And the fellow was only doing his best – it was a peace offering, honestly meant. She was sliding with his insistence, feebly submissive to it. Where was the woman in control of her own destiny? He stood up, dropping the cigarette tin into his shirt pocket.

'I'll give you ten minutes,' he said. 'Can't wait all night.'

The Diamond of the Raj was a new place in a side street off the city centre. It was the sort of street where the ownership and function of the shops were continually changing, never quite able to attract the custom of the stores on the main thoroughfares, just yards away. Even Myra knew that this place had until recently been a wallpaper shop. Now it was decked in maroon drapes, the ceiling covered by a light blue satin canopy drawn up to a big glass jewel in the centre. The staff, all beautiful Indian boys, were thick on the ground, braced for the onslaught of a Saturday night, this night, like Saturday nights all over the world, with waves of young men, laughing girls, sedate married couples, rowdies from the suburbs, all in pursuit of the varying states of oblivion available to them, according to their tastes.

Alex mused over the menu, ordering a prawn dupiaza with an affected authority to which the waiter responded with admirable restraint. Myra asked for chicken korma and when it came she ate dutifully, not really hungry, each mouthful inducing a little nausea which she hoped would go away. Alex was not helping, wolfing his meal, waving his hand in the air to order more lager. He said little else, fidgeting and turning round to watch the arrival of gangs of young people, here to claim the city centre for the night.

Myra had hoped to go home after the meal, but Alex insisted that they went to a bar he knew. This was a noisy disco-type pub, its smoky air shafted with laser lights. It was the sort of place, Alex explained above the racket, where 'faces' came to be seen. And to see what other faces were there.

'Good place, this. Very new,' he yelled in Myra's ear. 'I'm impressed. Nearly as good as London.'

It was a theme bar, he bawled, though Myra was at a loss to know what the theme could be. She looked politely for clues, scanning the metal-framed posters of American jazz musicians, the fake saxophones hanging from the ceiling, an imported style, brought to York, wantonly impinging on its heritage.

'The thirties, see,' Alex said in a lull in the very un-thirties music. 'Liven up a bit, eh?' He tapped her elbow and went to the bar.

It was a poor moment for Myra, standing there among the bright young things, their clothes so carefully chosen.

Why hadn't she given more thought to dressing? She was wearing her chintzy maroon skirt, a black velvet jacket she'd had for years, the same cream tights she wore for work. Her plainness was making her stand out. Maybe she should have piled on loads of make-up. Maybe she would have enjoyed that. She looked around at the 'faces', half in defiance, wishing she had a drink in her hand or that she could think of a more relaxed way of standing, of letting go of her handbag strap. She let her hands drop but could only clasp them in front of her so that she looked even more demure and available for scorn.

And yet there were people of her own age here, some older, like a tall leather-jacketed man in the centre of the room, long white hair in a pony tail, a man who knew how to carry his age, refuting the generation gap between him and the two teenage girls he was chatting up. And there was a quite elderly couple jammed in one of the half-circle seats that ran along one wall. But they, like Myra, were silent, watchful, Swiss or Finnish tourists perhaps who had wandered in by mistake, not knowing the rules. Or maybe it was just Myra, domesticated Myra, street ignorant. She looked for Alex but could not spot him among the three-deep press at the bar. The unwanted meal was still solid inside her and she felt hot and faint. To counter the malaise she concentrated on the street she could see through the big plate glass window. A red double-decker passed, and beyond the closed shops she could see a bit of the bar wall. She focused on this, reassured by it, its indelibility, the points of interest it had for someone like her, an academic, a stranger here.

After a minute she began to feel better, the nausea lifting to a more tolerable ache in the head. She looked about the room again, at the smug smiles, the cherubic lips of those who believed the world was built for them – the able-bodied and the beautiful alone. Soon they would discover the ephemerality of youth, the limitations of adulthood, then maybe, if they could stand it, they might find the joys of life to be had from growing older. This Myra thought with a welcome conceit, her self-esteem returning as she went to a vacated space near the wall, leaning against it to watch all the bodies about her with heightened powers of analysis. And it was then that she saw Rowena and Kate.

They were sitting – how could she have missed them before? – in the half-circle seat next to the two tourists. Rowena was wearing jeans and a red check shirt filled with her spreading midriff. Kate was in a white smock top and short skirt. They had their arms linked and seemed engrossed in a conversation which required, at one point, Kate to kiss Rowena's cheek. This drew a smeared glare from the man sitting opposite them who seemed concerned about people watching. He sipped his drink, dragged on his cigarette, drank again. And when he turned Myra's way she saw that he was the man she had assumed to be David dressed, not in the biker's gear this time, but in a cream suit and white shirt. Rowena looked up, straight at Myra, but made no gesture of recognition, turning coolly back to Kate who was folding herself about her arm, resting her head on her shoulder. Rowena nuzzled Kate's ear and whispered to her. Kate looked at Myra and giggled, making a show of taking Rowena's hand and guiding it along her thigh and under her skirt. She blew a kiss to Myra, a gesture that made David wince.

Myra reddened, this hell-hole of a place outwitting her, closing the door on her again. Alex returned, arms aloft as he carried the drinks through the crowd.

'Sorry. Got talking to a mate. Great here, isn't it? You should see it when it's busy, I mean really heaving.' He followed Myra's line of vision. 'God, dikes. They get everywhere these days. Still, each to their own, eh?' The two tourists stood and left. 'Fancy a sit-down?'

'No.'

'Aw, come on.'

'I don't want to sit down.' She turned her back on her colleagues. 'Look, I'm going to the loo. All right?'

Alex tutted, but she was already making her way through the crowd.

In the toilet there was no escape from the noise. The music was relayed there through a disc speaker in the ceiling, Myra went into the cubicle, feeling sick. She leaned over the toilet, but nothing would come. The nausea had shifted deeper down and she would not force it. She came out and stood in front of the mirror to straighten her hair, compose herself. Two giggling girls came in, horsing around, pushing each other against the wall. Then Kate entered, marching up to Myra's side.

'Ro saw you first,' she said.

'Did she?'

'Yes. She's always looking at other women. Does she look at you much? Does she stare?' She pushed her face up against Myra's.

'Look, Kate. It's none of my business, I don't – '

'Maybe you just haven't noticed the way she looks at you.'

'Listen – '

'She can stare all she wants, as far as I'm concerned.'

'Kate – '

'Ciao.'

She left the room. Myra sighed, waiting for half a minute before going back to Alex. When she got there, Kate and Rowena had gone.

'I think I'd like to go,' she said.

'What? Oh, for shit's sake, Myra. Some company you are. Hardly said a bloody word all night – '

'Look, Alex, I'm a bit long in the tooth for this kind of place. It's just not me.'

'That's crap.'

Myra groaned. 'I'll leave you here, if you like. I can make my own way back.'

His angry look melted and he glanced regretfully about the busy room, gulping down half of his lager. 'All right, all right. Some place else? Somewhere quieter?'

'Yes, somewhere quieter,' said Myra, though she would have preferred to go straight home.

'Right then.' He took Myra's untouched drink from her and put it with his own on a precarious-looking shelf above his head. 'Follow your leader.'

14

The wind in Micklegate carried the sweet reek of the sugar factory, a mile away, at the height of its winter campaign. Alex sauntered along, a new mood already achieved as he led Myra through the clumps of people thronging the night-time streets. At Ouse Bridge she looked at the lights of riverside restaurants reflected in the black glossy water, and felt a little brighter. They walked on, across the town centre and away down a narrow alley to a half-empty pub. Here, among the genuine wooden beams and red plastic seats, the gentle muzak and the rattle of the fruit machine, Myra felt more relaxed, as if the rowdiness of the last place had been a baptism for anything.

For the first twenty minutes or so, Alex ignored her, entertaining himself by butting in on the conversation of four German tourists at the next table. He talked to them in a mock Nazi accent that embarrassed Myra.

'Zo, ve vin se var ziss vay, right?' He arranged the ashtray and beer mats on the table in front of the bemused visitors. 'Ze Herr Churchill, he iz too smart for you . . .'

Myra edged away a few feet, wanting to be alone, to let her thoughts about Kate and Rowena collect in her mind. She did not feel shocked, only prudish. And things might be awkward for her at work – there were still three weeks before the end of term and Rowena had already hinted at Myra being kept on for a while in the New Year. She had no idea how she might handle Kate. She would have to take it as it came. There was no point worrying about it now.

The Germans, who had remained remarkably good-humoured, left with Alex calling *'Auf Wiedersehen'* and giving the Nazi salute behind their departing backs. 'Sodding tourists,' he announced, drawing random withering looks from about the room. 'Without them we'd be all right, wouldn't we? Don't need then choking up the place. We're all right on our own in this town.'

The drinkers who had heard him turned their backs. No one wanted to listen.

'There was no need for that,' said Myra.

'Why not?' He finished the large scotch he had treated himself to, sitting there and grinning like the big dumb beast he was. He laughed even louder, compounding his oafishness, then went to the Gents with a rolling swagger.

Two men at the bar were looking at Myra, the way men looked at a woman alone, secure in their physical superiority, keen for an opportunity to be solicitous, vainly protective. Myra felt lonely, wishing John were there, a foil for these men and for Alex's stupidity. She had a husband, she wanted to declare. And she was missing him. Tomorrow she would ring John, first thing.

The two men looked away when Alex returned from the toilet. Now he had a new routine, hands held limply in front of him, head wobbling loosely. 'Well, g-gee, Mr T-Tracy,' he said. 'Brains. From *Thunderbirds*. Get it?' He laughed and sat down close to Myra. Then he put his hand in her bag, scrabbling for her purse. She grabbed his wrist and pulled it out, angry with him. He smiled and clicked his tongue. 'Just testing. Watch out, there's a thief about.' And he laughed again, hollowly.

'One more drink,' Myra said, wearily. 'Then I want to go.'

'Really?'

'Yes.'

'And where do you want to go this fine festive night? What little pleasures you got in mind for us, Myra?'

'I want to go home. You stay, if you want to.'

'I might, I just might,' he said tetchily, sidling away along the seat.

Myra brought the drinks herself, knowing he had to have at least one more. He had drunkenness in mind and it was probably the only thing that would appease him, for better or worse. She bought a large scotch for him and brandy for herself, the smell of which served only to remind her of her earlier nausea.

Alex drained his glass in two mouthfuls, wiping the last drop out with his finger.

'Right then. Off.'

'I haven't finished.'

'You wanted to go, we go.'

Myra sipped at her drink, feeling it burn her lips. She would never be able to finish it. She handed the glass to Alex and he drank it off, drying his mouth with his hand. Then he stood and made for the door. Myra followed, deliberately taking her time, maddened by his manners – she would not have let the children at school get away with such rudeness.

Outside, frost was in the air, damp and heavy. People were making their way to parties clutching Tesco bags full of plonk and tinned beer. Some of the women were wearing thick winter coats with flouncy short dresses underneath, while the young men were inexplicably braving the cold in their shirt-sleeves and narrow ties. In a shop doorway, two women were shouting at a drunken and befuddled-looking man. Alex put his arm around Myra's shoulder, guiding her along, holding harder when she tried to shrug out of his grip. In this fashion they hurried along Pavement to The Shambles, to King's Square, the pubs crowded to the doors, the blitzing beat of electronic music blaring from a high open window. Myra wanted rid of him. She wished she was already home, alone, where she would have a bath, a last drink, perhaps even ring John if it were not too late. She considered the idea of giving Alex ten pounds to stay and finish the evening off in town, if he wanted to. But as they crossed the Minster forecourt he stopped, laughing, pulling Myra to him and kissing her hard. 'No.' She pushed him away. But he was smiling fiercely, a man with a mind of his own. He grabbed her wrist and tugged her on until she had to run to keep herself from falling over.

'Alex . . .'

'Come on. A bit of a lark, for God's sake.'

'Alex, no . . .'

But he had already pulled her through the railing gates and into the shadows behind the cathedral. He gripped harder, dragging her into a dark recess beneath the ancient windows.

'This is stupid.' She was trying to muster a tone of plain indignation. 'I want to go back.'

'You'll like it here, teacher.' He giggled. 'A bit of history. Ours for the making.'

Myra looked back at what she could see of the floodlit forecourt. She should cry out, draw someone's attention. But nothing had happened. Nothing was going to happen. She would be making a fool of herself. And she had never screamed in her entire adult life. Her wrist was burning and she stumbled on a tuft of grass, but Alex held her up, pulling her close to the wall, feeling along its length until he found a small door set two steps down from ground level. Myra could see the grey symptoms of his face, his thick fist as he forced the door's handle down until it gave with a snap that echoed across the lawns. Someone would have heard that, surely. But the old buildings about the lawns appeared empty. She made a sharp effort to tug herself away, but Alex simply spun her around, hugging her from behind, half lifting her down the steps where he pushed open the door with their combined weight.

'No, Alex,' she said firmly. 'For God's sake, grow up.'

'Relax. It's all right. You'll like this.'

It was a small ante-room, the floor littered with ladders, planks, a dump of scaffolding. The only light came from a high slit window and the open door. Alex pushed her in further and let go of her to close the door. Then he had hold of her again, dragging her to a pair of big old doors opposite. He put his ear to them, satisfying himself that there was no sound to be heard from the other side. He laughed.

'This isn't funny,' said Myra, mustering all the authority she could. 'Let's go, before there's trouble.'

But he was not listening. He coiled his arms around her, rubbing against her, saying this was the only fucking place in the town worth doing it in.

'No. Oh no.'

He put his hand over her mouth. 'Quiet, stupid. You'll like this. You'll love it.'

He put his hand in the small of her back and ripped her blouse out of her skirt. Myra felt a rising panic she knew she must not succumb to. What was she doing here? How could she have allowed this to happen? The hours, the day that had led up to this moment slipped from her mind. Now he was whispering heavily that he was in control, he was the Ice Man and this was what she really wanted, what she needed. Myra felt her arms going weak. She tried to remember the dozens of times in her life when she had heard other women saying what they would do in a situation like this, how they would kick and yell. The fools, their naivety. He pressed his face into her neck and she strained away, looking up at the webbed ceiling, its linked points picked out with black wooden flowers. Perhaps if she gave in, if she could just let these few minutes pass without thinking? He pushed her down, catching her mouth with his head, pinning her legs with his knees and pushing up her skirt. She slapped his face, but the blow was feeble.

'Get off me, you bastard.'

'Tiger! Ti-gerr!'

Now, as he fiddled with his belt, her strength came back, fuelled by contempt, informed by her entire history of survival. God would provide, in this, His house, God would provide. And, as if in answer, as if her righteousness were to be divinely proved, she put her hand to her side and it fell immediately on a scaffolding angle. For a fraction of a second she tested its weight, an almost fatal hesitation since Alex looked down to see what she was doing. But she was too quick for him. Right was on her side. And, with her fury neat and compact inside her, she lifted the thing and banged it against his head. It was an act of surprising ease, almost pleasurable, though she was uncertain about its effect. He groaned and leaned back. 'My fucking eye. Bitch.' Myra drew the weight back and lashed out again, this time only grazing his cheek.

'Get away from me, you shit. Leave me alone.'

While he rubbed at the wound, inspecting his hand for blood, Myra wriggled from under him. Now she was standing, the rules had shifted in her favour. But she did not know for how long. He staggered to his feet. 'For fuck's sake, Myra . . .'

The door was to her left, ten feet away. He started blundering towards her. She was still holding the lump of metal, but she no longer had the weapon of surprise. The physical advantage had passed to him.

'That hurt, you know, Myra. That wasn't right . . .'

But his words were halted by noises in the cathedral, the sweep of torchlights that could be seen at the foot of the big doors, the main lights that were turned on in the nave and choir. Alex turned to look, wobbling. And Myra ran, knowing this to be her cue, reaching the small door in three paces, dragging it open with the last of her strength.

Seconds later she was back on the streets. The time scale of the day, the evening, had become grossly misshapen. Such was her alertness, it could have been morning, a fresh day, work in half an hour. She looked around, at a taxi queue across the road, at a few lads clowning about at a hot dog van in front of the art gallery. A young couple walked by, arm-in-arm, paying her no attention. She shook her head and squeezed her eyes tight. She opened them again, the night alive around her, her mind racing with wild streams of logic. What could she do? What were the rules in situations like this? Her blouse was torn, and her lip hurt. But she had not been violated. The boundaries were unbroken and it had not been tragic, not an event to add to the blacker archives of history. Yet it was still wrong. In Manchester she would have known what to do, where to find the police station to stand among the other Saturday night casualties from the pubs and clubs in Ancoats, Strangeways. But not here. She did not know this place, she did not belong. A police car shot by, under Bootham Bar towards the Minster, and she walked instinctively in the opposite direction.

Within ten minutes she was home. She turned on the lights, the heating, and dried her face. She had wept all the way back, without really noticing it. Still in her coat, her hands and whole body shaking, she laid the fire in the lounge, needing the heat, the flames. When it began to take she put the guard round the hearth and went for a bath, lying there a long time until the shaking had finished. Putting on her thick robe she went downstairs. What if Alex came back? She would not have the strength to deal with him again. She would have to rely on the rules of the house, the return of the old order of landlady and lodger, on his coming to his senses. But she was too tired to think about it – her weariness imparted a strength, a healthy indifference.

With a stiff whisky she sat down on the sofa, staring into the raw throat of the fire, as she had so many times, as she had when she was a girl full of dreams about what she would do with her life, that time connected to this by a fine straight line. All along that line she'd come, a human racing, knowing days of exultation, of hope, fears of illness, aberration, all taken in her hurtling stride from mother's womb to this, one day to nothing. Soon. Too soon. Where did the time go to?

Her mother still travelled that long line, here to there, A to B to Z. Myra wanted to think about her, to have her in the room to hear her daughter's thoughts, taste her anger, slow her mad passage through time. She entered into an imaginary conversation with her. Men were bastards, all of them. And her mother agreed, reinforcing Myra's comments with tales of her own. And John? Was he a bastard too? Maybe. Yes, maybe. If he had been here, none of this would have happened. Bastard. Selfish. Where was he now? Tomorrow she would make plans for moving, back to Manchester, or even to her mother's house in Southport. Back to square one, to give up this mad racing existence. Going back. Regression. Enough of starting a new life. It went wrong, it always went wrong. The old times, she wanted the old times back, in a place where she had been young, known happiness, where she could grow old and forget this lousy night, this town, forget too the events that had brought her here, in winter, in flight . . .

∫

15

The yellow gorse receded on the hills above Pawnton and the land acquiesced into the formal blues and browns of autumn. With the garden tamed and the last of the leaves burned, John reluctantly told Danny he did not think they would have any more work for him until the spring. The boy accepted the news with a shrug and disappeared to his end of the village.

During September and October Myra had applied herself vigorously to the redecoration of the house, keen to impress their personalities on it; she had visions of being holed up there for weeks on end if the winter months proved harsh. Until then she would admit to having only average homemaking abilities; her time had always been taken up with work. But she surprised herself with her efforts, her increasing confidence with coloured paints and wallpaper, the imaginative siting of things from their old house: the earthenware urn in the corner of the lounge, the miniature copper tea set on an alcove shelf in the hall. Then everything stopped when Laura was bedridden by a mystery virus.

The local doctor was alerted. He was a tall nervy old man called Friar who had worked this practice for thirty years. He was mystified from the beginning, returning daily, taking endless blood samples as if during the time between each visit he had hit upon some new random idea about what it may be. Myra fretted. Laura was listless, white, taking only morsels of food that Myra could hear turning in her stomach. There was something in her daughter's blood, a bad visitor. By the fifth day, although the lethargy seemed to have evened out, John suggested moving Laura to a private clinic in Manchester. Myra agreed and immediately began packing for both her and Laura. But by the time John had arranged for the day off work and at the very moment he was booking a room at the clinic, Laura came shakily down the stairs, demanding her breakfast. And by the afternoon, she had shaken off the wobbles and the room was cancelled. In the evening Dr Friar arrived. He examined her and stood back, saying, 'Children. What a worry!' And he smiled, positively dewy-eyed with relief.

Laura was already the right age for nursery school, but there was nowhere local, and besides Myra wanted these last few months alone with her, snatching at the time, this long holiday from the modern convention of an endless working life. Motherhood was beginning to suit her, as she never thought it would, and she quietly nurtured the possibility of another child. It would, somehow, confirm the existence of the first. She made plans for the following year, a tender scheme she would put to John soon.

With the winter taking hold, they did not feel inclined to wander too far from the house and, with Danny out of the way, Laura claimed the garden for herself, making a den between the end wall and the new shed. It was a place, she said, just for her. 'No adults allowed. Right?' Myra nodded gravely, appreciating that children, like adults, like animals, needed a space they could control. As was the habit of only children, Laura invented imaginary friends, one of whom was a Mr Do-Nothing, a hybrid of the men she had seen in the village who, like Danny, were out of work and spent long hours apparently idle. She took the role of

Mrs Do-Nothing, lecturing her husband about his laziness, about his getting under her feet all day and 'spending all night in the pub, the bloody, bloody pub.' Myra thought this hilarious, though she was careful to take the game as seriously as she could.

In late November, mid-afternoon, the phone rang. It was Abigail, an old student friend whom Myra hadn't seen for years – she had been slow in sending out change-of-address cards and had only recently posted the last and lowest priority ones to occasional acquaintances like Abi. She was her usual scatty self, and though it was good to hear her voice again Myra found it oddly intrusive, a link with the old life, the rat race she was allowing to run off without her. But she listened politely as her friend told her about the fashion design course she was taking up, the teaching she would never, could never, dear, go back to. Every few minutes Abi stopped to let Myra offer a few spare details about her own life, then she would interrupt her saying how amazing it all sounded before breezing on to her own existence again, the fresh boyfriend, the flat she had in Sale. The time passed and Myra thought she heard Laura in the kitchen, knowing she would come in any minute now, hating the dark, a recent phase that had meant them leaving both her bedroom and the landing lights on all night. When Abi had finally exhausted her supply of news Myra half-heartedly invited her out to the village for a weekend some time and was at last able to put the phone down. Then she went out through the open back door to find the night, cold and fully arrived, the garden empty.

Her first feeling was one of unfolding space, a wild sense of the world, all it consisted of outside her own physical province. Myra didn't exist, she was somewhere else, she was every rock and blade of grass that was in the darkness in front of her. And she wanted that, to be the distant world that held her missing daughter, not to be the one who was, in this moment, solely responsible for Laura not being there. At first she held the panic in, something that could wait while she searched the garden, the old Myra, the loving mother calling gently for her scamp of a daughter, secretly keening for a simple solution that would mean an evasion of the dire void opening inside her, hoping for the passage of time that would see them in the evening, gathered about the table, Myra, John and Laura, who were suddenly distant beings in her mind's eye, foolish, conceitedly unknowing creatures whose faces she could not recognise, especially her own.

Laura was not hiding in the den, or the shed. It was not a game. As Myra ran back up the garden path, the new, stupid, useless path, the world flooded into her, her tears unstoppable as she searched the house, one empty room after another, every stick of new furniture, every strip of cottagey wallpaper suddenly vile and naive. Laura. How could she not be found in the very next second? How could relief from this moment, from the entire universe that was crushing Myra, that she had always trusted blindly, not be possible? She ran back down the stairs and grabbed her coat, her mood changing to one of anger, a powerful force with which she would conquer the outside world to its very last corner.

She ran out and round to Mrs Malt's, banging on the front door. Laura would be there, of course, playing under the table, teasing the dog, warming her hands by the old kitchen range. Mrs Malt opened the door. Laura was there, wasn't she? Her baby? Let her have her back, now. But the old woman shook her head. The spite, the witch. What kind of game was she playing? Joe waddled into the hall behind her, telling Myra to come inside while he rang the police. But she didn't want to go inside. She wanted to stay out there in the world where her daughter was. Couldn't he see that, the slow old fool? And then Myra was knocking on every door in the row, heedless of the mad self she was revealing to everyone, people she barely knew, who spent their lives keeping a polite distance from each other. Look. Start looking, Myra yelled, crazed by their hesitancy, her own mind burning with every inch of the village's geography.

Men appeared from the houses, pulling on overcoats, testing torches. They made their way to both ends of the street, some smiling thoughtlessly as they passed Myra, frozen now in the arms of a woman she had not met before, letting the men carry her madness away with them. Then officialdom arrived to make a genuine case of it all – a policewoman and a constable first, followed by a detective who led Myra back to her house. There, time mortifyingly took on its familiar passing quality. Myra tearfully answered questions about what Laura was wearing, who her friends were, where she liked to play, anywhere that particularly intrigued her, details that seemed banal, yet which required a horrible precision in their telling. The detective gently asked if John was Laura's natural father, if there had been any marital problems, anyone they had had an argument with or who might bear a grudge, questions that put before Myra's mind the whole unacceptable lore of child abduction. The woman, who said her name was Sally, put her arm around Myra, explaining that they had to rule out the possibility of this being a 'custody' case.

The two men went out to their car. Myra had the feeling that the whole village was gathering there. Then the constable returned, saying they had tried to get hold of John but he had left the office. Myra sat at the table with Sally. In another life they might have been about to play a game of cards. The policewoman took Myra's hand, awaiting the best moment to put a few more questions to her, carefully withholding any false optimism about how it might all work out happily, soon.

Then John arrived, walking into the horror that Myra had created, having to deal with her first, the new fit of crying that came when she saw him. He was still outside the event, incapable of taking it in, of course. And he spoke quite calmly with the constable who had come in with him. On his way into the village John had seen Danny, running from behind the Heritage Centre. Maybe he could help? Maybe he'd seen her?

And maybe he had.

A minute later the senior officer came into the room, ushering the constable away, but nodding to Sally that she should stay. For a moment Myra felt annoyed with them, a stray domestic anger about the way they had commandeered their house as a base for their operations. It was their home. It was not to be treated that way. Then she saw the look in the detective's eyes and pitied him, knowing his fate, what he had to say, his dreadful duty in having to impart the news that they had found Laura, that he was so sorry.

And when he had finished speaking, time no longer passed but simply gathered about them all, moment on moment . . .

Myra woke up, the cinders sliding in the grate, the black into the red, coal to flame to smoke. To nothing. She had been dreaming that she was John's father, in a room in the attic, listening to the sounds of the house below, the closing of a door, a telephone ringing, familiar ritual sounds some distance removed, in a time-scale that was somehow physical, existing independently at her side. There was a flurry of activity in the street, an argument between people she knew but could not name. Someone was trying to get in, to *save* her. But no one could get in her way now – a certain thought, the last sure effort of intelligence. She was dying, dying for John's father. She could see the window of the room, the heaps of his belongings, a suitcase, an old coat, objects in which she had no interest, which knew nothing of her passing, this full and light dissembling, the rising into a personal space. The end of the room was miles away and the sky was above her, the seasons wreaking their tyranny on her body. And then there was only air, its substance momentarily everything, before the falling into nothing that had woken her up.

She had not died. She was still human, still racing. But not saved, not safe from the memories she still had to face. She had a sudden fantasy about being back at her mother's house. That was where she had to go, back to being a child again, back to the womb, the melting pot, and further, to beyond the dawn of history.

Her head ached and the arm on which she had been lying had gone to sleep. Her coat was still draped across the arm of the sofa. She reached for it and pulled it over her, lying down on her good side, watching the last of the fire, the window for the arrival of morning. Her mother's voice eluded her so she invented imaginary friends, those indulgences of the only child that Laura had been, that Myra herself was. They understood, they knew what she had been through . . .

She spoke in her head, telling them about Laura, about her being found in a ravine behind the first hill on the moors. They'd had to identify her in the back of an ambulance. Couldn't they have thought how awful that was? But it didn't end there. It couldn't, could it? Maybe they'd had it coming, some sin to pay for, as John thought then, as he thinks now. The police went looking for Danny. They found him in a barn at the top farm. There'd been some suspicion about him in the past, an incident with another child. Nothing proven, but in a place like that . . . They arrested him and took him away.

Danny, the bringer of the storms that flew up from the moors and smashed on the roof of the house while Myra wretchedly clasped and unclasped her arms about the child she had lost. It was the worst of all nightmares, so terrible it could not be true. All the nights of Laura's tiny life when Myra had watched her in sleep, listening to her soft breathing, terrified it might stop. All that vigilance, all that fear suffered and stored that the unthinkable might never happen. And yet it had. Myra died in herself. Maybe she was still dead, and now she should realize this, that she must always grieve, that she was vain in hoping she might ever live fully again . . . She remembered the slowly passing days, the storms that ripped the shed and the gazebo to pieces. John hardly seemed to notice this, withdrawing from the pain, the glass bubble forming around him, encasing him in ice.

The pathologist did not help. He kept delaying his final report, something he couldn't put his finger on, the signs being that Laura might simply have fallen down the ravine. But how could she have got there on her own? Danny was in custody, saying nothing. They call it 'awaiting charges'. And while everyone was trying to make up their minds a few drunks were brought into the cell next to his. They were full of hell, refugees from that hateful world that tells them what they must want, what they must eat, own, fuck, without which they can never be happy. Maybe they'd seen the news on television, or some perverse officer had dropped the hint about Danny. Whatever, an argument started about them not wanting to spend the night with a child-killer. There were scuffles, a riot, they got to him . . . Myra never knew the full details, except that Danny had been stabbed and did not recover. And charges could never be brought against a dead man.

It was a year ago, almost to the day. They'd tried to stick it out. Christmas came, the worst of times when they had planned to stay with Connie but the snow had come and blocked all the roads from the village. At first, John seemed simply quiet, stoical, but he was only holding it back, standing aside, staring at his sadness as if it was a geometric principle, an architectural design he could not taint with his natural feelings. He began saying it was his fault for being so friendly with Danny, for not spotting the signs. He blamed himself for their leaving Manchester, which didn't help when the villagers turned against them. No one spoke. Someone pushed dog shit through the letterbox. And Danny's father crawled into a bottle. From being victims of a tragedy they were transformed into figures of hate, Myra and John, the newcomers who had brought all that upset.

In January, Bill was taken by the silence and John sank further into his cold self. He never went back to work. In a crude moment he said he was applying for a job as a street cleaner. It was what he wanted: to be down in the gutter, among the filth. Myra summoned what strength she had left, telling him they must go, must run, anywhere. John revived a little, a single day of rationality in which he made a few calls and found out about the job in York. They would be near his father. They could have his house. Connie was certain not to mind. Myra wasn't at all sure, but there was no alternative. They had to get away, to be free of the moorland air that had turned to poison in her lungs. And so they came, in winter, in flight from the past . . .

But you never truly escape it, she thought. It just holds you and holds you and you cannot break free.

16

The street outside was quiet, as if everyone had moved away, or the four-minute warning had gone up and no one had bothered to tell Myra.

It was past midday, the sun crossing behind the terrace opposite. Perhaps it would be fine all day, the light cold and clear, the kind of winter light that could lend a timelessness to the most banal scenes: the railway yard with its piles of rusting machinery, the sugar factory and its chimneys trailing white smoke to the heavens. Myra closed her eyes again. She was still on the sofa. Her head felt woolly, her limbs weak. She would stay there until these feelings passed, until the energy came of its own accord, the body putting itself to rights. And the head. She would not be going back to her mother's. She would never leave John. She saw him with her inner eye, watching the way he flinched, feeling the hurt he still carried, that she had denied herself, too soon, too soon. Her, Myra, seeking salvation, claiming the winning side without thought that there had to be a loser: John, the victim, taking their pains in a double measure. They would heal the wounds, they would talk, an endless stream of words, Myra would insist on it.

A noise came from the room above, someone stirring, footfalls progressing about the upper floor. Another ghost rising, coming down the stairs now, standing in the doorway of the lounge, holdall in hand. But this ghost breathed, had flesh, and a crepe bandage over one eye.

'Myra?'

'Go, Alex.'

'I just wanted to say, you know, sorry.'

'Just go.'

'I mean it. I don't know what happened to me. I feel bad, really bad.'

'Go.'

'No, look . . .'

He remained for an interminable time, the boy, standing there, imbecile that he was. Then he turned and closed the door. Myra saw his shadow pass the curtained window, another storm over, moving away, to be forgotten.

The day passed readily. She stirred herself by mid-afternoon, making coffee and a sandwich, but she could only manage a few mouthfuls, the bread dry in her mouth, falling undigested in the pit of her stomach. She was still tired, fatigue breeding fatigue, so she went to bed, to let the body be still, her thoughts be still, the night to pass over her.

The next morning, plain blue. It was seven thirty and night still had its grip on the skies. Winter was firming up its hand, but the world was strong, resilient, exerting itself against the pressure of darkness. Myra rose, her blood moving, oxygenated. John had not rung, or if he had, she had not heard him. This afternoon she would ring him, tell him that Alex had walked out – that would be enough – and that she was missing her husband.

She turned on the radio, welcoming the news, every scrap of it: the latest unemployment figures, the discovery of an IRA bomb cache, an imminent U-turn on education policy. Myra absorbed it all, the comings and goings, triumphs and disasters – she appreciated every jot of information with a keen and receptive interest. She was part of it again, part of the world. She showered and dressed for work, hungry to be there. With a few minutes to spare she looked in Alex's room. He had thrown the duvet over the bed, closed the wardrobe door, a feeble attempt at tidiness, a gesture perhaps, of remorse. But he really had gone, and even his usual fusty smells were already fading. An hour's work in there this afternoon would see the last traces of him tidied away for ever.

The night had retreated by the time Myra drove out to the school. Now the sky was an even grey with a hearty wind nudging the bare trees, lifting the girls' skirts, the kids walking backwards into it as Myra pulled into the car-park. She was actually five minutes late and she entered the building just as Andrew was calling the children in for assembly. Rowena was in her office with two other women as Myra passed by to put her coat in the staff room. On her way back, Andrew came into the corridor, smiling, the last of the children scurrying in about his legs.

'Who. . .?' Myra pointed her thumb at Rowena's door.

'Supplies. Tell you at break. OK?'

But Myra did not need to wait that long to find out what was going on. Ten minutes into the working day, Rowena came into her classroom.

The children had been slow to settle, sensing something in the air, but this did not seem to worry Rowena as she looked calmly down at them, ruffling the fringe of one of the travellers' kids.

'News,' she said to Myra. 'If you're interested.'

'Should I be?'

'Maybe.' She scratched her lip. 'It's Kate. She's gone. For good, it seems.'

It was an invitation. She was opening the door on last Saturday night, wanting to explain. Or was she? Myra wanted only to work that morning, not to have to suffer revelations or feel obliged to take sides in an affair that did not concern her. She stared straight at Rowena, forcing the older woman to look towards the window and the playground with its sapling borders.

'What do you mean, "gone"?'

Rowena winced a little, lips firming piquishly.

'Vamoosed. Her and the boyfriend. Touring the world for a year. A sudden decision, I believe.'

She was keeping cool, perhaps hoping for Myra's sympathy and support.

'Oh. I see.'

'Well, it can't be helped. And the thing is, there'll be a vacancy. There was going to be one anyway. Some national learning audit's put the authority in the top four in the country. There's money in the pipeline, apparently. Lucky us. So, what do you think?'

'Sorry?'

'Come on, Myra.' She pushed her glasses up the bridge of her nose, still looking out of the window. 'Do I have to spell it out? Let's say I'm strongly advising you to apply for the post.'

'Oh, right.'

'I'd like you here permanently. You're good for the place. Reliable. We need some stability round here. Think about it, won't you?'

'I will.'

At morning break, out of hearing of the two new helpers, who seemed in great need of each other's company, Myra mentioned the offer to Andrew.

'Great. You take it.'

'But what if Kate came back?'

'Too bad. If she's said she's going, she's out, and that's that. Can't say I'm sorry, personally. It was always rather awkward, her being here.'

'How do you mean?'

'Her and Rowena.' He leaned forward, glancing at the two women who were deep in conversation. 'They had, how can I put it, something going between them. Only Kate couldn't quite make her mind up about herself. Before this guy it was the man from the gas board. She used them to taunt Rowena with. Rather cruel, if you think about it. You must have had your suspicions.'

'Yes. I suppose I did.'

'You apply,' he said, sinking back into the armchair. 'You'd be great. Things might start to work round here, at long last. God, Christmas, I think I'm rather looking forward to it, for once. How about you?'

By lunch-time Myra felt tired again and she was glad she did not have to work on the nativity play that afternoon. The offer of the job was something she could not think about. She could easily turn it down, finding some excuse about looking for a different kind of work. Teachers did that, quitting the classroom to open a sandwich bar, become hotel receptionists, fill shelves at Kwik Save. It was the pressure, the strains they all knew about that held them together or drove them apart. But she could probably stand it, she knew. And full-time jobs were hard to come by, these days. When John came back she would discuss it with him, see how it might fit in the plans for a new beginning that she had in mind for them both.

Back at the house, she decided to ring the nursing home then ring Connie to see if John was still there. But as she was about to pick up the phone she heard a click in the kitchen. At first she thought it was only the heating cranking up, or a piece of furniture cracking, as it did in the night. She went back along the hall and looked around the kitchen, seeing nothing amiss. Then she checked in the pantry and saw a thin bootlace poking out from between a box on the floor and the white emulsioned wall. She slid the box aside and saw it, the tiniest creature, perfectly dead, the gin wire imbedded deep in its skull, drawing one minute black eye down to its snout. A drop of blood was already congealing on the wooden base. So John had not imagined it. Myra leaned over to pick the mouse up with the idea of disposing of both it and the trap together. But she decided to leave it for John to find, for the small satisfaction it might give him. Then, as she was sliding the box back with her foot, the phone rang in the hall.

'Myra?'

'Yes?'

'It's Connie. John's sister.'

Myra paused to let the husky voice be married to the picture she had of Connie in her mind – appealingly plump, bustling, capable.

'Oh, hello. Great minds, Connie. I was just about to ring you.'

'Were you? It's not about Dad, is it?'

'No. Well, I haven't been in touch with the home yet. I'd intended to do that before I rang you.' For some reason she was affecting a businesslike air, as if she was in the middle of a hectic domestic schedule.

'I see,' said Connie. 'I had been wondering. John's so forgetful these days. It's over a week since he phoned.'

'Is it? Are you . . . are you sure?' Myra turned the phone's flex in her fingers, trying to straighten out a coil. She did not want to have to say this. 'He's not there, with you I mean?'

'No. Should he be?'

'He . . . he said he might visit you, that's all. He's in the area on business.'

'Well, if he's coming, he hasn't turned up yet.'

'No, obviously not,' Myra said, forcing a nervous laugh.

'Look, I'll ring the nursing home and see how Bill is, then I'll ring you back. All right?'

'Yes. OK, if you say so, Myra.'

Myra put the phone down and went into the lounge, a tightness in her scalp, her empty stomach aching. She went to the sideboard drawer for her packet of cigarettes. There was only one left. Alex must have been helping himself to them. She took the cigarette out and lit it, feeling an immediate wave of nausea. She took two more drags and stabbed it out.

It seemed wise not to have made too much of her not knowing where John was, though Connie was aware of his distractedness and may well suspect something was wrong. Myra put the thought behind her and, for the hundredth time in this past twelve months, she gathered her wits about her, thinking carefully about where John might be, his state of mind when he had left on Saturday morning, so long ago, it seemed.

With no other plan coming to mind, she rang the nursing home. The understanding Shirley answered, though Myra was not sure if she was grateful for this – the self-absorbed young man might have been easier to deal with. She asked how Bill was. Shirley replied with a few clichéd details about his being 'rested' and 'comfortable'. And alive, thought Myra, relieved that her failure to ring yesterday had not mattered. Then, uneasy about having to lie, she commented that John had intended calling to see his father over the weekend before attending to the same 'business' Myra had invented for Connie's sake. Shirley paused, no doubt incredulous that a husband and wife should be so poor at communicating with each other. Her mind would be working overtime, suspicions of an affair, a break-up, the middle classes about their business of cool deceit. John had indeed been to see Bill, she said. He had come Saturday morning and stayed until late in the afternoon. Quite a chatterbox, John had been. And him so reserved, usually. Now Shirley was spilling the beans with relish, taking the wife's side, fuelling whatever problems she thought they had. When she had taken the evening meal in she found John had propped the old man high up in the bed, saying excitedly that it would help him breathe, that his colour was improving, remarking that some of the things Bill had been saying made sense, if only people bothered to listen properly. Then John had talked about his daughter. Shirley didn't know they had a little one. But then why bring her to a place like this, goodness knew what nightmares it might give her. Shortly after, John had left, rushing out into the night without so much as a word. That business of his must have been urgent, she said with a chuckle.

Myra thanked her and put the phone down, tired of her suspicious voice. She went back into the lounge, thinking the world a big and empty place, where she was alone again, deprived of a future, of the passing of time which was suddenly slow and laboured. She could not think clearly. Who else might she ring? And what had John been saying about Laura? She struggled with the idea that this might develop into an incident.

Ten minutes passed. Then half an hour. She was angry with John, mad *about* him. She put the radio on for the news, but the only talk was of pit closures, of Princess Diana's visit to Nepal. But what was Myra expecting? News of an accident, or some coded message such as the insane are supposed to hear? She turned the thing off and found herself once more in the big slow silence that was becoming an affront to her, the enemy of logical thought. The female newsreader's voice was still in her head, the lisp, the casual undertone of a woman who had heard it all before.

Myra went upstairs and changed into jeans and a jumper. She was going to do something, to try and find John. If something unthinkable had happened, she was not going to be found here, the useless housewife, the limp recipient of a bad news item that might barely stir the attention of an indifferent newsreader.

17

The sun was low, a big yellow eye in a parting of the clouds, burning through the windscreen of Myra's car. She drove through Harrogate, Skipton, watching it dipping to her left.

Her resolve was up for constant review. What if John had gone home, or was trying to ring her? Why had she never agreed to their having a car phone? And if she went all the way to the village – where else was she heading? – what would she do there? Who could she ask about John without stirring old wounds, without making a monumental ass of herself? At some point she would have to consider calling in the police. But surely that would never be necessary. It seemed so extreme.

She continued along the moors roads, the shadows deepening in the valleys, the reservoirs black and shiny like oil slicks on the bare green land. Open country, empty country, the cars and lorries sped along the road as if their drivers feared being caught in the endless spaces about them. The return journey might not be so easy and even if she turned round now, she would not be home before early evening. For nine miles she followed a saloon car with a sticker in the rear window – 'A Woman's Place Is In Control'. The car turned off at a roundabout and Myra was left with open road.

The first appearance of the village's name on a motorway sign made her mood sink. She turned off and followed the quiet road through the hills. The day they had left Little Pawnton she had not looked back, following the removal van up the steep narrow lane that led out of the village. She had decided she would never go back, never even glance at the name on a map. Now she resented John for drawing her here, a foreboding growing inside her as she got closer, Laura's presence all about the hills, her sad ghost locked there in each knoll, each stone, each house, as if she could not be dead, as if nothing died but simply hovered in its resting place, suspended in time. Myra blinked away a few tears. She had a silly idea that she might pretend to be a visitor, denying any previous knowledge of the streets she was now cruising through, thinking like a tourist as she viewed the cottages, how homely, the church, how quaint. But it was not working.

The main street was deserted save for a young woman. Myra had not seen her before, and it gave her hope that time had passed, that there was fresh blood in the village and old memories were fading. Her attention sharpened and she looked for signs of John's car, though her anxiety was still there, playing games with her as she struggled to remember the car's colour and make. It was silver-grey, of course. A Volvo. She missed the turning to their old street and had to pass almost out of the village before she found a driveway big enough for her to turn around and go back. She felt a wave of sickness and she wished she had a cigarette, knowing she would tolerate one beneficially this time. At the top of the main street she turned and went down the narrow linking lane to the next road which she followed to the junction at the end.

The house was visible now, its For Sale sign miraculously untouched in the weedlocked front garden. Myra had wanted so badly for it to be sold, but no one had been near it for months as far as she knew. She wondered about this, about the neighbours alerting prospective buyers to the house's sad history. One day it must sell. Everything sells, eventually. Thinking about this distracted her for a few moments as she drove to the end of the row and round the side of the house that faced open countryside. There she found John's car. It was a Volvo. And it was white.

She took no satisfaction from the fact that her instincts had been right. He was here, somewhere, but she couldn't bear to think beyond that. She looked up at the tiny square bathroom window, the only window on that side of the house, but there was no sign of life. She got out of the car, put on her jacket and slammed the door loud enough for it to be heard inside. Emboldened by the sound, she found the one key they still had for the house and went round to the front door, feeling large and obvious, trying not to look for the prying eyes there might be at the window of the Malts' house, or the bungalows opposite and further down. The lock was stiffer than she remembered it, but it gave with a second firm twist.

Behind the door was a heap of junk mail, a few yellowing free newspapers, and two or three legitimate letters addressed to her and John. She tried the light switch, even though she knew the electricity had been disconnected. There was no response, the hall and the rooms beyond remaining forbiddingly dim. She knew she had to close the door for the benefit of anyone watching who might suspect vandals.

'John?'

Her voice was weak, her throat dry. She ran her tongue round her mouth to moisten it.

'It's me, Myra. John?'

The air was damp and acidic. She took a deep breath and went into the living-room, making her movements deliberate and brisk, as if she were simply returning from a trip to the shops. But her breath was held inside, and her thoughts were static, avoiding the blackest of possibilities. The room was empty. She went back into the hall. The moments seemed insurmountable, and it was against her frozen will, against time, that she made herself go forward to the kitchen door, leaving her natural self somewhere behind her. The glass from one of the back door panes was scattered on the floor, the door itself half open to reveal the woolly garden and a magpie preening on the end wall. This scene, the space of the garden, was an irresistible contrast to the confines of the house. Myra took a few steps into the kitchen and found muddy streaks in the sink. She tried the cold tap. The water shuddered the plumbing and gushed out. The supply had been turned on outside. She was about to go into the garden when she heard a single soft brushing sound on the bare floorboards of the room above.

'John? Hello?'

But there was no reply.

She went to the foot of the stairs and called again, using the same 'hello', the only word she could find in her entire vocabulary. And when there was no answer, she went up.

In what used to be their bedroom, she found him, sitting beneath the window, the room having a fruity smell, like old booze or urine.

'You shouldn't have come. I didn't want you here.'

He was not looking at her, but Myra could see the stubble on his face, the grey hollows under the eyes, the pallor and wear that had come with just two days on the loose from the kindnesses of domestic life. But he was alive. For this she should give thanks.

'I had to find you. I was worried.'

'No need.' He gave an ugly chuckle. 'No need to worry. Not about me. Plenty worse off in the world than me.'

He was drunk. He stirred, shifting his weight from one side to the other.

'Come home, John. Please?'

'Home? Where's that then?'

'You know very well.'

'Do I?' He made to stand up, staggering against the wall. 'This was our home once, remember?'

'Yes. I remember.'

'Our dream home. Our dreamy dream home.'

'John . . .'

'Fuck the dreams,' he said, standing, wobbling. 'If it wasn't for fucking dreams we'd be all right. We'd never have come here.'

'That's not right. What's the point in thinking like that?'

'Because I do. Because it was all my fault. All . . .' He made a sweeping gesture with his arm. 'All this.'

'It was not your fault. It was no one's fault. If anyone was to blame, it's me.' She did not want this talk, it was awful, it would lead nowhere. But she could think of no way of diverting his train of thought. She felt cold, standing there. She wanted to touch him, but she knew it would be the wrong thing to do. 'You seem to forget that day. I was the one who wasn't watching her.'

Her. The great foundation presence in their lives, her name unspoken for so long, unspeakable. Laura. Maybe if Myra used the name it might help. But there was a broad empty space between them. A year, and they had said virtually nothing about their daughter. Now it had come to this.

John took an unsteady step forward, shaking his head.

'It's so easy for you, isn't it? You can just . . . forget.'

'I can't forget. I'll never forget,' Myra said, angrily. 'You have to go on living, that's all. It's why we're here, to live our lives, make the best of them, for others as well as ourselves.'

'Smart words.' He looked at her, waving his finger.

'Lovely, lovely words.' Then he snorted, blinking his eyes wide open, brushing past her to the landing. He stopped at the top of the staircase then clattered down, falling over three steps from the bottom. Myra ran down after him.

'For God's sake. John, what are you trying to prove?'

He picked himself up and laughed, rubbing his knee.

'Let me take you home,' said Myra, daring to put her arm round his shoulder. 'Please? Before you do something you'll regret.'

He groaned, pulling away from her, going through to the kitchen where he splashed his face with water from the tap.

Myra followed. She could do nothing but follow.

'I'm calling it a day, Myra,' he said, wiping his chin with his sleeve.

'What do you mean? Don't say things like that.'

'I've had it. Done for.'

'You're not "done for", John.' She was almost shouting, her exasperation getting the better of her. 'You've got a future. You've got me, family, a decent job. It's life. It can be good. Why can't you think about these things?'

He grinned sourly, but Myra felt a glimmer of success. She was getting through to him. He had lost face, that was all. And that wouldn't matter to her. It would remain a secret, their secret, he would know that. But then, unbelievably, he turned and lunged at her, some other person, a beast in pursuit of a great calamity, a fool who pushed her over and ran through the back door with a roar.

Myra fell on her hand, wrenching her wrist.

'John! Don't just run off! John . . .'

She scrambled to her feet, but by the time she reached the door he was already beyond the garden wall, running across the pasture land to the first hill.

'John! Please . . .'

Myra rubbed at her wrist. It hurt, it might be broken, but she had no time to think about it. She stepped into the garden then began running, awkwardly, half tearfully, straddling the wall and chasing over the misting winter grass.

18

Beyond the garden wall and the rough track that ran behind the houses was a bramble hedge, and beyond this was dry-stone wall country, the moor in winter where the sheep picked among the heathers and mossy scree, where they would stand and let themselves be buried by snow if the farmers did not get to them first. Higher up was the line of weathered crags and standing stones that watched over the valley at the other side. The clouds were gathering about this near horizon so that its outline was uncertain, emerging occasionally in the fading daylight, then disappearing in a puff of mist.

Myra tore the sleeve of her jacket getting through a gap in the hedge. The cold dew on the grass penetrated her canvas pumps within half a dozen strides. And blood was filling the tissues in her hand. But she had stopped crying. Now she was sustained by a grim urgency, a duty to catch up with John, a belief that this was what he really wanted her to do. Her efforts were further fuelled by the many rehearsals in her mind of how she might once have pursued Laura up here. But the fact that she was making that journey now, the reality of it, was too horrible to contemplate and she simply kept going, borrowing emotional energy from the future, a debt to be repaid some other day.

Ahead, night was claiming its territory, though the wind

was behind her, carrying a few stray sounds from below: a dog barking, a tractor making its way along the lane at the north end – the village about its small business, enviable, detestable, in one and the same breath. She reached the shale that the rains brought down to the grassland, losing a shoe. She ran on a few steps barefooted, cursing since she knew she had to go back to retrieve it. As she fiddled with the lace she saw John's silhouette, two hundred yards up. He was making his way between two huge columnar stones.

'John!'

But he did not stop.

Myra's head was hot and full, the adrenalin failing, her lack of fitness shaming her. For a split second the memory seeped back of her usual quiet identity, of the entire line of events that had brought her to this moment. She pulled the jacket tight about her, carrying on to the bigger stones, her progress slower as she felt tentatively with her toes for the small crevices hidden in the shadows. Her skin and breath were cold, as if her body was dissolving in the damp air. But the energy was coming anew, drawn from days beyond this, when there might be hope, time to unravel this latest and unwanted knot, if she could just get to John and stop him doing anything stupid. And that was the word for it. Stupid. Selfish, the fool. It was almost useful for Myra to think of him this way.

At the standing stones she slowed, picking her way between them, catching her breath. At the other side was a limestone pavement, the stones white and contoured like rows of molar teeth. A three-quarter moon was rising and away to the west, three miles away, were the lights of Turton, the next village. Nearer, between the limestone flats and the next distant hill, was the black scar of the stone valley. Myra walked across the pavement where there was an odd pocket of warm air, the wind thwarted by the crags behind her. She drew breath to call out, then decided against it, not knowing the value of her voice in this space, the effect it might have on John, wherever he was. She looked around for him. They might have been a courting couple playing hide and seek.

When she reached the end of the pavement, she saw him. He was standing above a forty-five degree incline that dipped to a sheer drop into the black valley bottom. Her chest ached and her mood dipped again. This was no game. She looked for the way down from the pavement, fearing her own panic. The only route she could see was a small turning pass that would take her out of sight of John for a few seconds. It was a chance she would have to take. She clambered down through the pass and out on to a narrow sheep path that ran along the top edge of the incline.

Now she had few ideas, save that she wanted John to see her. From somewhere came the idea of feigning injury, like the bird who will pretend it has a broken wing to draw intruders from its chicks. But it would only trivialise the moment, any calm authority she might bring to bear on the situation. Despite her real cuts and aches, her wrist pulsing with pain, she put her hands in her jacket pockets and walked as casually as she could to within ten yards of her husband.

'I told you not to come.' He was looking down into the valley, then up at the far horizon. 'I didn't want you here, Myra.'

'Well, I am here. I can be here if I like,' she said, evenly.

'It's over. I'm finished.'

'So you keep saying.'

He straightened his back, taking a deep breath, his footing established on his heels. Myra took an involuntary half-step to her side.

'I didn't want to do this to you, Myra.'

'Then don't.'

'I didn't want you to know . . . to see . . .'

'Well, I can walk away, if you like,' she said, still calm, though her heart raced as she realised she was gambling with every inflection in her voice. 'Do you want me to go?'

He closed his eyes and turned his head to the sky.

'I . . . It's just so pointless. Empty. I'm empty. There's nothing in here. I'm nothing. I . . .'

But a rogue breeze took away the rest of his words.

Myra felt a rush of anxiety that she had to keep in check. She sat down on a stone at her side, wiping it first with her hand, hoping to defuse some of the tension with this minute ordinary action.

'It's because you won't let anyone get close to you, John. You just shut up shop and push people away. People need each other.' Her words were puerile, but they came anyway, an instinctive filling of the void. 'You can't do it all alone. You can't live without help from other people.'

'Don't. I don't want to know.'

'No one wants you to hurt yourself, John. Me, everyone, we all only want what's good for you. Can't you see that? Can't you let yourself see that?'

An aircraft was passing high above, a jet on the climb for its short hop from Manchester to Amsterdam, or further, Moscow perhaps. Its noise imparted a sliver of reality, a brief reminder of the human race about its business. But John noticed nothing. He never did.

'Everyone thinks the world of you, John.' The repeated use of his name was deliberate, to remind him of himself, the good man he really was. 'I've never heard anyone say a bad word about you.'

'They don't know what it's like being me. No one does.'

Wallowing. That was the word for him now. But Myra knew it would be a mistake to use it.

'It can be better. You've had a bad time. You're depressed . . .'

'I've a right to be.'

'And haven't I?' she said with a measured impatience, a wild card played that caused him to drop back on his haunches. This startled Myra, though her heart had a reconciliatory beat now, taking care of itself, unalterable, whatever happened.

'Look, John. I love you. I need you. What more can I say?'

'You don't. You don't need me,' he said, with a wrench of anger. 'You'd be better off without me.'

Myra sighed, suddenly tired, as if the whole thing was slipping from her grasp and she could do no more to stop it, could want to do no more, her lassitude fatal, unbeatable. But she had to fight it. Perhaps now might be the right time to go and sit beside him, though her reason, born of God-knew-what wisdom, told her that the initiative must be his.

'It was down there,' he said.

'I know.'

'That's where they found her.'

'Yes. I know.'

'A year ago. You didn't come and look, did you? You didn't bother.'

'I didn't need to,' said Myra, wearily. 'I couldn't. What would have been the point?'

'Someone had to see.'

'Look, I cared just as much as you. I still bloody care. But this isn't the way to prove it. You go on living. You make good of life. That's how it's done, John.'

'One step, over the edge. I could join her.'

'That's ridiculous.'

'A movement of the foot, begins with the leg, here . . .' he said, with a revolting laugh.

'Well, do it then!' she yelled, getting to her feet. 'Go on. Do it! Just don't blame me. You've brought it all on yourself. Don't bloody blame me!'

Myra began walking back to the pass up to the pavement, the tears flowing freely, all conscious will, all tension abandoned. No one to witness this, no one to believe her efforts, one more dreadful secret, one too many . . . At the rocky gap she turned. John was back on his feet, swaying in the twilight, taking half a step forward and testing his purchase on the slope with his heel. No one to know this, no one else to care . . . He leaned his weight forward again, lifting his hands to his head. No one to see . . . Now he was moaning, rocking carelessly, tripping in a half-circle down the banking, falling over. 'Dear God,' Myra's whisper. Then she could not see him.

She ran back along the path, seeing nothing along the length of the slope until his head appeared, a grey disc in the shadows.

'Myra? Myra? Help me?'

She slithered down the grass banking, loosing a single stone that came to rest on the edge, ten feet away. He was lying on his front. She took hold of his arm and pulled him to his feet, some merciful angel ensuring that the ground was firm beneath them as they scrambled the rest of the way back up. On the safety of the path he fell into Myra's arms, a heavy wretched load.

'I wanted to hurt myself. I wanted . . . to be damaged.'

'All right.' Myra kissed him hard, holding him hard, trying to impress her warmth and being on him, all that she could offer. 'Over now. It's over.'

'It'll be better?' He was shaking, squeezing the flesh of her waist till it hurt. 'Promise me it will be better?'

'I promise.' She lifted his hands and kissed them. 'I'll help you. If you'll let me.'

John nodded, eyes closed, face screwed tight. He opened his eyes and stared back down the slope.

'Don't look,' said Myra. 'Don't look back.'

And she helped him up the path and through the rocks at the top of the hill. At the other side, mist was collecting, cloaking the village so that only the church tower and the roofs of the bigger houses were visible, all of the same violet colour, floating in the air.